Beater Cottontail

BUNNY FOO FOO

BOOK #2

E.V. DEAN

CONTENTS

PROLOGUE

Sisters In Secrecy

The creature in the woods had Marie Lavoie's eyes and her husband's temper, which was why she never missed the nightly feeding. Not in thirty years. Well, only once, and she'd deeply regretted that mistake. She'd fed him through blizzards and hurricanes, even the night she broke her hip. But tonight, sitting in the Rusty Fox with her third beer, Marie was about to make that same terrible mistake again. And this time, it wouldn't just be her own life at stake.

St. Patrick's Day was one of Marie's favorite holidays. And given that she was turning eighty in a month, she knew there wouldn't be many more of them left. When her husband Paul died three years ago of emphysema, Marie made it her mission to live life to the fullest, there was no other option.

She lived in a small colonial house on the west side of Berlin, New Hampshire, nestled near the foothills of the mountains. At her age, she was beginning to worry that her son might take away her independence. Things moved slower now, her bones ached, but she still believed she was sharp as a tack. The thought of being put "in a home" terrified her.

Marie had responsibilities at home, ones she feared her son would never understand. If she told him even a fraction of the truth, he would be absolutely furious. Not to mention, he was the Chief of Police in Berlin. God forbid he found out what she was up to, not only would he be upset, he'd be morally compromised.

So, she didn't tell him.

In fact, she'd kept the secret for decades.

This St. Patrick's Day, Marie planned to meet her friend Martha at the Rusty Fox down on Main Street for burgers and beers. It was their tradition, one Marie cherished even more now that both of them were widows.

They sat at the long mahogany bar, drinking McUltras and talking about the latest episode of *Grey's Anatomy*. It was their special show, they'd watched every season together for over twenty years and loved every minute of it. But *Grey's Anatomy* wasn't the only thing the old women bonded over; they shared a few other curious similarities.

Marie and Martha had both moved to Berlin with their young children around the same time, some fifty-odd years ago. Martha came from New Brunswick, and Marie from Quebec. They were both Canadian.

And they were both witches.

Yes, real witches!

They didn't ride broomsticks or have long, crooked noses, but they were connected to something larger than themselves. God or the Devil, to be quite honest, they weren't entirely sure. But both possessed special talents they couldn't explain to anyone in Berlin except each other.

They kept it from their husbands.

From their children.

From everyone, except one another. It made them sisters in secrecy. And now, as they grew older, they feared the day they'd lose each other, because when that happened, they would also lose the only person in Berlin who truly understood them.

But on this particular St. Patrick's Day, Marie and Martha got a bit too carried away. They were older now, and they underestimated the effect of half a dozen McUltras on their aging bodies. Time at the bar began to evaporate. Minutes turned into hours. Everything moved slower. Jokes were funnier. The ticking clock on the wall seemed to disappear entirely.

It was a rookie mistake.

Something Marie wouldn't have done if she hadn't been drinking. She usually reserved alcohol for birthdays and holidays, but this time, things had gotten a bit out of control.

Before they knew it, the handsome bartender, Mack, a childhood friend of Martha's son, came around for last call.

"Last call?" Marie asked, startled. She looked up at the clock. It was ten o'clock at night. Her head had just started to spin, slow and heavy.

Martha turned to Marie, panic spreading across her face. "Oh my god."

"He's going to think we abandoned him," Marie said, her voice trembling.

Martha quickly reached into her purse and tossed some cash on the bar. They struggled to get off their stools, both woozy, both doing their best to walk straight out the door. But they had to move, and fast.

They were late. Very late. For a very, *very* important date.

· · · · · · · · · ● · · · · · · · · · ·

Martha agreed to come home with Marie. It was an emergency, after all. You see, it had been ages since Marie last forgot to handle her nightly responsibilities. By now, it was a tried-and-true routine. Every evening at dusk, Marie would step outside her little colonial with a picnic basket full of food.

It didn't matter if it was raining, sleeting, snowing, or sunny, each night, she entered the woods at the same time and waited.

The only other time she'd forgotten, years ago, it had been a disaster. So terrifying, in fact, that Marie had nearly sworn never to return. But something in her heart pulled her back. Guilt, perhaps. A deep sense that she owed him.

So on this St. Patrick's Day night, Marie and Martha walked arm in arm into the woods, gripping the picnic basket as their bodies trembled in unison. By the time they reached the treeline, they were already four hours late. And they knew, he would be angry.

Violent, even.

"Crazed," was how Marie had described him the last time.

But that was years ago. And she was younger then.

Now, neither of them was sure they could handle him if he turned violent again.

The pair stood beneath the towering trees, the darkness pressing in around them. Moonlight filtered weakly through the canopy, casting just enough glow to see a few feet ahead. Beyond that, nothing but blackness.

Marie swallowed hard and glanced at her friend. Martha nodded, a silent gesture of understanding, as if to say: *I'm sorry, friend, that we're even in this mess. But it's our life.*

"John," Marie called out into the forest, her voice unsteady.

Typically, he would already be there, waiting for her. She'd chat with him for a little while, hand over the picnic basket full of food, and he would disappear into the trees. By morning, the basket would be left in the same spot, ready for her to refill for the next night.

Her voice echoed through the woods as Martha gripped her arm tighter.

The last time Marie was late, he'd been furious, belligerent, even. Cussing, screaming, spewing rage like he'd completely lost control. His eyes had turned bloodshot, tinged with a crazed yellow glow. He shouted so violently, spit flew from his mouth.

Marie had been so terrified that she dropped the basket and ran, tears streaming down her face. The guilt never left her. She had made him this way. She had confined him to the shadows of the forest.

Because she was afraid of him.

Her own goddamn son.

It had actually been Martha's idea, all those years ago.

After he did what he did, it had felt like the only way to let him live. Otherwise, John would've spent the rest of his life locked in a cage, a young, broken man wasting away behind bars, never to be free again.

So Martha and Marie did what they had to do.

"John, are you there?" Marie called out.

Only silence answered, along with the wind whipping through the birch trees on that cold spring night.

Had he left?

Was he furious?

Marie had no idea. But one thing was certain: his absence was more terrifying than the tantrum they might have faced had he shown up.

She was frightened of her own son.

Marie knew a truth that would destroy her if she ever spoke it aloud. The grim reality was that John wasn't entirely her son anymore. The spell she and Martha had cast all those years ago had worked too well, binding something dark and evil to his flesh. What began as a desperate mother's attempt to save her child from prison had become something far worse than any cage could contain.

The townspeople of Berlin had no idea what stalked their forests. When pets went missing, when livestock vanished, when children reported seeing "a big white dog" watching them from the treeline, they blamed coyotes or bears. They had no idea there was something far more deliberate. Something that studied their routines, learned their weaknesses, and marked the most vulnerable for future meals.

Marie was the only barrier between John and the innocent families of Berlin. But she was eighty now. Her body was weakening. And the creature she had created was only growing stronger, hungrier, and more cunning with each passing night.

What John would do in the coming weeks would be worse than anything he'd ever done before.

And it was only just beginning.

Little Sandy Sommers would vanish as John's hunger grew stronger, disappearing so completely that even the search dogs would lose her scent at the edge of the forest. The only trace left behind was a single Easter egg, cracked open and empty, found where the hiking trail met the deep woods. No footprints. No torn clothing. No signs of struggle.

As if she had stopped existing altogether.

Little did Marie know that this St. Patrick's Day night would spur a change in her son. Her nightly offerings would no longer be enough to satisfy what he was becoming. Something far more terrible had taken residence in his heart, something that moved like a predator and knew exactly how to lure the innocent.

John had never been a good boy. He'd never had the chance to truly become a man. And the apparent rejection by his mother that night would push him into becoming something else entirely.

John would no longer wait for Marie's picnic baskets.

He had learned to hunt.

And when little Sandy followed what she thought was the Easter Bunny into the woods, she tumbled down a rabbit hole with no way back up.

CHAPTER 1

Celebrations

Chief Lavoie sat at the long oak table, surrounded by members of his extended family as they celebrated his mother's 80th birthday. It was getting late. Dinner was over, and everyone was still picking at their dessert. Chief Lavoie was on his second helping of birthday cake, his favorite strawberry cake, the one his mother's best friend Martha made every year. With cream cheese frosting, he couldn't get enough.

Despite the cheerful party and the chorus of birthday songs, something felt off. Maybe it was just the general malaise that had settled over Berlin in recent days. A child had gone missing. The city was now at the center of a massive investigation. And quite frankly, Chief Lavoie didn't know what to do.

Nothing usually happened in Berlin. Certainly nothing like this.

The small mountain town had devolved into a frenzy of media chaos in just a matter of days.

In his decades as a police officer, Chief Lavoie had mostly handled the occasional drug bust, burglary, assault, or petty crime. Now, he was facing the disappearance of Sandy Sommers, a sweet little girl with bright blonde hair and rosy cheeks. She was only six years old. And at this point in the investigation, it was highly likely that Sandy was dead.

Chief Lavoie didn't tell anyone that, of course. But as a law enforcement officer, he knew the truth: if someone wasn't found within the first forty-eight hours, chances were they wouldn't be found at all. And according to witnesses, poor little Sandy had wandered off into the woods.

And the woods of Berlin, New Hampshire, were not kind to anyone, especially not to a little girl.

As Chief Lavoie looked down at his phone, he noticed dozens of missed messages. Technically, he probably should have stayed at the station, but how often does your mother turn eighty?

Speaking of which... where was his mother?

He narrowed his eyes and looked around the table. She'd been gone for quite a while now, and he needed to leave soon.

He turned to Martha, his mother's best friend, who sat on his left. "Martha, do you know where Mom is?" Growing up,

Martha had been like a second mother to him. She and Marie had been inseparable from the moment they met.

Martha shrugged. "I think she went outside to feed the chickens," she said with a small smile. "You know how she is. Has to feed those goddamn chickens at eight o'clock or else all hell breaks loose."

Chief Lavoie rose from his seat and patted Martha on the back. "I'm going to go outside and look for her. I've got to head out and get back to the station."

A flash of panic crossed Martha's face as she grabbed his chubby hand. "No, no, honey. We just started catching up! We have so much to talk about. I need to know the inside scoop on the investigation. All my friends at the club knew I was going to see you today, I can't go back without any gossip!"

Chief Lavoie shook his head and adjusted the leather belt on his uniform, straightening his holster. "No, unfortunately, there's a lot going on with the Sommers case. I don't really want to talk about it anymore, Martha. I've got to get back to work."

Before Chief Lavoie could turn away from the table, the doorbell rang, echoing through the small colonial house.

He frowned and made his way down the hall. They weren't expecting any more guests. In fact, half the party had already come and gone by now.

When he opened the door, he was surprised to see a tall Black man with glasses standing on the doorstep. He wore a flannel shirt and khakis, his round glasses resting low on the bridge of his nose.

It was Otto Finch, the Mayor of Berlin.

"Chief Lavoie," Otto said breathlessly. "Is your mother home?"

Chief Lavoie narrowed his eyes. "She's out back feeding the chickens. Is everything alright?"

Otto shook his head. "Unfortunately, no. It's not alright. We need to talk. I think your mother might know where Sandy Sommers is."

CHAPTER 2

A Friend

Marie sat just inside the forest, perched on a tree stump, her body trembling. She wiped the tears from her eyes and glanced down at the picnic basket at her feet. It had been over a month since St. Patrick's Day. Over a month since she'd seen John. And with each passing day, the knot in her stomach grew tighter. She knew, deeply, that something was wrong.

Still, she came out here every night, hoping and praying to see him peek through the brush with his long white ears and soft voice, not that harsh growl he used when he was angry.

Sometimes they'd sit in the woods for hours, just talking. Marie would update John on the family, and John would describe what it was like to live among the trees. Since that fateful day when Marie and Martha cast the spell, John's world had become painfully narrow. He was completely confined to the forest. That was by design. If he stepped beyond its threshold, his body would seize in agony, forcing him to buckle and collapse back into the trees.

When Marie and Martha made that tragic decision all those years ago to punish Marie's wayward, dangerous son, they banished him, through magic, to the borders of the Berlin forest. It was the only way to keep everyone safe.

But if someone wandered into those woods and happened to stumble upon John, in whatever state he was in that day... well, that was on them.

Over the years, Marie often worried that John was still up to his old ways. One summer, about ten years ago, a horse had accidentally escaped its pasture and wandered into the woods. The owner found it weeks later, barely recognizable. It had been skinned, every strand of hair gone. Its eyes and hooves were missing, and large chunks of flesh had been torn away. The story made the rounds on social media and in local Facebook groups, but most people chalked it up to the old farmer spinning tales.

Marie knew better.

When John was younger, he'd had an unsettling fixation with skinning squirrels. He was only eight at the time and had just gotten a BB gun for his birthday. One day, Marie's husband, Paul, walked into the woods and discovered a cluster of trees strung with tiny, dripping pelts, John crouched beneath them, his small hands slick with blood, wearing the largest skin like a glove.

And now, as Marie sat on the stump, she couldn't stop thinking about that poor little girl whose face she'd seen again and again on WMUR. Sandy Sommers, who had wandered into the woods one Easter day during an egg hunt and never came back.

She couldn't bear the thought that maybe it was John who had hurt Sandy. After all, it was his recklessness with children that had led to his punishment in the first place.

The last time Marie and John had truly talked was a few days before St. Patrick's Day. As usual, John sat hidden in the bushes while he spoke to his mother. Even after all these years, Marie knew he was ashamed of his form. She never asked about it, never pushed him to step beyond his comfort zone.

"What are you going to do for your birthday this year?" John had asked from the shadows that night.

Marie always made a conscious effort to look into his glowing yellow eyes. Even if she couldn't see the rest of him, she did her best to make eye contact.

"Oh, you know, nothing fancy. Haven't really thought about it. It's still winter, and you know how the weather at this time of year affects me. I can't think more than a week ahead. April seems so far away," Marie said with a small laugh. It was still cold in New Hampshire, snow blanketing the ground.

"I think you should go somewhere warm. Like Miami," John said. "You deserve it."

"Ha... me in Miami? With what, a little umbrella in my drink? How ridiculous. I wouldn't even know how to get there! I guess your brother could help me. Maybe."

A low growl escaped from the bushes, but Marie brushed it off. Any mention of Nolan made John bristle. His hatred toward his brother frightened her, and she worried every day about what might happen if the two of them ever crossed paths out in these woods.

John quickly changed the subject. "Guess what, Mom," he said.

Marie sat up on the stump, her hands tucked into mittens and folded across her lap. "What?"

"I made a friend," John said.

A friend? The words made Marie's chest tighten. In all the years John had been banished to the woods, she had never heard him mention a friend.

"Her name is Lily," John continued. "She's really nice. We've been talking for a while."

Marie began to shake her head. "I don't know, John—"

"She's never seen me," he said with a small growl. "And she never will. She just sits on the edge of the forest and... we talk."

"Talk about what?" Marie asked.

"You know... I just tell her about what goes on in here. The animals, the mountain, how to live in the woods all by yourself."

Marie took a deep breath. She didn't want to ask the next question, but she had to. "How old is Lily, John?"

John didn't respond. He shifted in the bushes.

"John?" Marie pressed.

"It's not like that," he muttered.

"Then what is it like?" she asked.

"I'm lonely," John growled. "The only one who talks to me here is you. Sure, maybe you bring Martha over sometimes, but I can't keep living like this."

Marie bit her bottom lip and began to rise from the stump. "I should go. I'm getting cold."

"Mom," John said. "Please, don't be like this. It's fine. It's not like that at all. It's the mayor's daughter, for Chrissake."

Marie's eyes widened. She couldn't believe what she was hearing.

"John. I beg of you. Don't ever, ever talk to me about this again. If you do, I'll never come back here. I gave you Nicholas. And now you're just being greedy."

John growled, his nose twitching.

Marie knew all too well how much John hated when she brought up Nicholas. She mentioned him often, driven by guilt over the whole ordeal. But it was never enough for John. He always wanted more, no matter how much it cost his mother's conscience.

"Greedy? You don't understand what it's like, being in here. Stranded. It's torture."

Marie shook her head. To her, it always felt like John was pushing her buttons. Asking more and more from her until she was forced to compromise her own morals.

And now, as she sat once again on the stump, staring into the empty forest and praying for her son to reappear, she realized just how wrong she'd been that night.

She should have spoken up.

She should have said something.

She should have stopped this before it started.

And on her 80th birthday, Marie was beginning to accept a terrible truth: what was happening in Berlin just might be her fault.

CHAPTER 3

Witches

O tto couldn't stand the way Chief Lavoie looked down at him, standing in the doorway of his mother's house, eyeing him like he was a pest. A little bug just waiting to be squashed underfoot.

But the truth was, Otto had something very, *very* important to tell Berlin's Chief of Police.

He could feel sweat gathering on his forehead, his blood rushing hot through his veins. He'd just driven all the way from Dr. Brighton's house outside of Boston, gripping the steering wheel so tightly he thought it might snap. He'd floored the gas, rocketing up Interstate 93 and winding his way across the Kancamagus Highway through the mountains to Berlin.

The moment Dr. Brighton told him that the creature he'd seen in the woods was likely created by a witch of French Canadian descent, Otto had started putting the pieces together.

There were plenty of French Canadian families in Berlin, but one stood out, more vocal, more proud than the rest: the Lavoies. And if Otto were a betting man, he'd wager everything he had that Chief Lavoie's mother was a witch.

Not because she *looked* like one, of course. Truthfully, Otto didn't even know what a witch was supposed to look like. What convinced him, almost beyond doubt, was history.

When Sandy Sommers went missing, Chief Lavoie told Otto that this was only the second time in Berlin's history a child had disappeared. The first was over thirty years ago, when Chief Lavoie's own brother, John, vanished without a trace. John had been older than Sandy, sixteen at the time, but still a child.

Except when John disappeared, no one in town seemed particularly upset. In fact, according to Chief Lavoie, most were relieved.

"My brother was a demon," the Chief had told Otto one late night as they sat in the police station, trying to piece together anything they could about Sandy's disappearance. "You know, I don't even think the force really looked for him when he went missing. Everyone in town hated him. Loathed him. Even me. I was just a kid, I think I was eight… maybe seven, and I came home from school one day and John had…"

Chief Lavoie swallowed hard under the fluorescent lights of his office. He paused, staring off into the distance, before turning back to Otto with a flicker of sincerity in his eyes.

"I think he killed my hamster. It sounds silly, I know. It sounds insane. But I got home from school that day, went into my room excited to see George, that was my hamster's name, my best friend at the time, and he was gone. Except for his head. His head was sitting in the cage, staring up at me with those beady little eyes… and I never recovered."

Otto swallowed hard, his eyes dropping to his hands. "Your brother did that?"

Chief Lavoie nodded. "He claimed it was the cat. I never believed him. His life was full of fucked-up shit like that. So when he disappeared, everyone, except my mother, was almost elated…"

"Can you take me out back to see her?" Otto asked now, shifting in place. Nolan was older, stronger, and bigger than him, and after all these years, Otto still found him a bit intimidating. Even though Otto was technically his boss, he had to remind himself of that now and then.

Chief Lavoie leaned against the doorframe, gripping the wood with his meaty hands. "What is this about, Boston?" he growled. "Anything you can say to my mother, you can say to me."

Otto takes a deep breath and clenches his fists. "You're going to think I'm crazy, Chief. You're going to think I'm completely insane."

Chief Lavoie shakes his head. "Just spit it out, kid."

Otto bites his lower lip and forces the words out. "I think what happened to Sandy may have something to do with your mother."

"Finch," Chief Lavoie growls.

"But it's more than just your mother. I…I think your brother is alive."

Chief Lavoie's eyes widen. "You've got some nerve coming to my mother's house on her birthday saying stupid shit like that. I don't want to hear it."

And right in front of Otto's eyes, Chief Lavoie slams the front door.

But Otto doesn't fret.

In fact, he refuses to take the Chief's "no" for an answer. If Chief Lavoie won't help him figure out what really happened to Sandy Sommers, Otto will have to take matters into his own hands.

He begins circling the outside of the old colonial house. When he reaches the backyard, he spots the chicken coop tucked into the far corner, just at the edge of the forest. To the left of the coop, he sees an old woman sitting on a stump, fiddling with her hands.

Otto starts walking quickly through the damp grass as the evening dew soaks his shoes. His heart pounds in his chest, he's never met a witch before. Not that he knows of, at least. As he walks, he can't help but think of *The Wizard of Oz*, when Glinda says to Dorothy, *"Are you a good witch, or a bad witch?"*

Surely, a woman who turns her own son into a demented creature cannot be a good witch, can she?

Although, if Chief Lavoie's brother is as terrible as he made it seem, perhaps she could be a good witch after all.

When Otto reaches Marie, her back is turned to him as she holds herself in her spring jacket.

"Mrs. Lavoie?" Otto says.

Marie quickly turns around to face him. Her face is red and puffy, and tears stream down her worn and wrinkled cheeks.

"Mr. Mayor," she says, her voice shaking. "What are you doing here?"

"We need to talk," Otto replies. He swallows hard and looks down at his feet. "But first, I have to ask, are you okay?"

Marie takes a tissue out of her pocket and rubs her eyes gently. "I... I'm okay. I think. You know, I turned eighty today, and it's hitting me harder than I anticipated."

Otto nods and looks out toward the forest as the sun sets. Night is approaching, and he cannot stand the thought of being in the woods after dark again. Especially without a gun. Especially without Clementine, the sharp FBI agent who had given him all the courage he needed to run headfirst into the dangerous woods the first time.

When Lily went missing and wandered into the forest, Clementine was Otto's rock. She helped fuel his bravery. That night, they confronted the creature together, surviving only by the small mercy of the beast. Otto cannot imagine facing it alone.

Otto nods empathetically. "Marie, I need to ask you something important, and I hope it doesn't offend you. That is not at all my intention, and whatever you say will stay between us."

Marie lets out another sob, signaling to Otto that she may already know exactly what he is about to ask.

"Are you a witch?" Otto asks.

Marie looks off into the distance toward the woods and begins to nod slowly.

"And your son, John, is he—"

Marie opens her mouth to speak, but a rustling in the brush interrupts them.

Otto's heart drops as Marie rises from her seat on the stump. Deep in the thicket, just beyond the clearing, the bushes begin to bristle. At first, the movement is quiet, then it grows louder. Whatever is in the bushes is large, larger than a mountain cat, judging by the way the trees shift and bend to make way for it.

"You should go," Marie says, grabbing Otto by the arm. "You need to go. Now."

Otto swallows hard and plants his feet firmly on the ground. "I'm not going anywhere, Mrs. Lavoie. I know."

Marie looks up at Otto with her worn, panicked eyes.

"Your son... I think he kidnapped Sandy Sommers."

CHAPTER 4

Brotherly Love

When Chief Lavoie looks out the kitchen window and sees Otto standing at the edge of the woods talking to his mother, something rages inside him. He can't stand that stupid mayor sometimes.

While Otto may be from Berlin, just like Chief Lavoie, he carries an air of pretension. Unlike Chief Lavoie, Otto went to all the right schools. He started off at Robin State College, the best public college in the state, then made his way to Northeastern University and climbed the ranks to become one of the top real estate developers in Massachusetts.

Simply put, Chief Lavoie is a bit jealous of Otto, and it infuriates him when the mayor directly defies his orders. Sure, Otto may technically be his boss, but Chief Lavoie feels like he is Berlin to his core. Otto, in his opinion, is not.

The mayor has a fancy house up by the edge of the mountains, a nice car, and money. He doesn't understand the real Berlin way of life like the Lavoies do.

So when Chief Lavoie sees Otto once again disobeying him, he storms out of the house and into the backyard. This time, he is determined to teach Otto a lesson once and for all.

It doesn't matter if he gets in trouble for it. Enough is enough.

With his blood boiling, Chief Lavoie stomps through the cold spring grass as the sun begins to set, his eyes locked on Otto.

"FINCH!" Chief Lavoie yells across the dewy grass.

Otto snaps his head around in shock, his eyes wide as he shakes his head. "No, Chief. Don't—"

"What the hell did I tell you, kid? Leave my mother out of this!" Chief Lavoie growls.

But when he reaches his mother and Otto, standing at the edge of the woods, the anger in his body quickly fades and turns into confusion.

Tears are streaming down his mother's face.

He grabs her by the shoulders. "Ma, what's wrong?"

Before she can answer, a rustling comes from the bushes at the edge of the clearing. It's loud, so loud it makes his stomach flip and his head snap toward the woods. Was it a bear? A mountain lion? Rumor has it that wild boar roam this part of New Hampshire too.

"We should get out of here," Otto says, stuttering.

Marie shakes her head. "No. I need to see him. I need to apologize. Maybe I can stop all this."

"Ma, what are you talking about?" Chief Lavoie asks.

Marie breaks free from her son's grasp and begins walking toward the clearing. "John? Is that you, honey?"

John?

Chief Lavoie's blood runs cold. It can't be. Not John. Not his twisted, deadbeat, creep of a brother who was better off gone; because, damn it, he was supposed to be dead. He'd been gone for almost thirty years, and Berlin was better for it. All that bastard ever did was bring the Lavoie family more harm than good.

Maybe it's nerves, but something makes Chief Lavoie reach for the gun in his holster.

"John," Marie says gently. "You can come out now. It's alright. They know. They know about you."

Chief Lavoie turns to Otto. "What do you know that I don't?"

Otto begins to stutter and stammer as the bushes rustle again. Whatever is out there, it's massive. Maybe it's a moose? Or a buck? Judging by the weight of its steps, it has to be at least one hundred and fifty pounds.

"Mom, you don't know what's in there!" Chief Lavoie yells. He draws his gun and points it toward the bushes.

Marie shakes her head, tears streaming down her face. "I do, honey. It's your brother. And I've been lying to you for a very, very long time. I'm sorry."

Otto shakes his head. "Marie, I didn't tell you this part, but I don't think your son is well. He's sick. Something is wrong with him. He's deformed, angry... violent." He looks at Chief Lavoie. "He took Sandy. He admitted it. And he tried to take my daughter too."

Marie freezes and turns back toward Otto. "He did?"

Otto nods. "He's been talking to her in the woods for months. Trying to get her to come with him to the tunnels."

The rustling grows louder until it's clear to all three of them that whatever is in the bushes is only a few feet away.

Chief Lavoie cocks his gun and holds it steady, pointed at the source of the noise. "I don't care what's in there. I don't care if it's my brother or a mountain lion. I don't want to know. Especially if it's that bastard."

"Nolan, please..." Marie cries as she steps toward him.

But it's too late.

Chief Lavoie pulls the trigger. The bullet rockets through the air and tears into the brush, striking the creature with a loud thud that sends it collapsing to the ground.

CHAPTER 5

Grounded

Lily Finch is as angry as any little girl could be. She sits in her room, staring out the window at the deep, dark forest that lines her backyard. On her arm is a long, fresh gash from where that thing scratched her.

He was supposed to be her friend.

Her *Best Forest Friend*, to be exact. But when she walked into the woods last night, searching for his help and guidance to find her friend Sandy, he attacked her.

In all the times Lily sat with BFF in the forest, he was never angry or aggressive, and he never showed his true form. He simply sat in the bushes, talking with her about life and what it was like to live among the trees.

Now, Lily sits in her bedroom, very, very grounded, as her arm throbs in pain. It was her fault, after all. She had thought it would be a good idea to ask BFF for help finding Sandy. Instead, she learned it was BFF who hurt Sandy in the first place.

When she got home last night, her father yelled at her like he never had before. She didn't even know he *could* yell. In all her few years, he'd never so much as raised his voice.

As her grandmother cleaned the gash and wrapped it in a bandage, her father paced the kitchen, spiraling.

"Why would you go into the woods?"

"Why didn't you tell me you were talking to someone in the woods, Lily?"

"Didn't I tell you not to talk to strangers?"

Poor little Lily just sat there, taking in every word from her father, trying her best to keep her composure; when, in reality, she felt deeply betrayed. Her Best Forest Friend had lied to her, and all she wanted was to find her real best friend, Sandy, and bring her back home.

· · · · · · · · ● · · · · · · · · · ·

When Otto watched Chief Lavoie fire the gun into the bushes, his chest tightened. When they had tried to shoot the Fool, the name by which he'd come to know Marie's son, John, in the woods, it had been completely useless. The creature had still towered over them, walking step by step closer as if the bullets hadn't even hurt it.

But this felt different. After the gun fired, whatever had been lurking in the bushes collapsed to the ground with a loud thud.

Marie let out a long cry. "How could you?!"

When the Chief walked up to the brush and pushed the bushes apart, he shook his head and turned back around.

"It's a deer," Chief Lavoie said. "A buck."

Otto quickly walked up beside him and saw the buck lying on the ground, shot in the chest. But he saw something else too.

On its left side were three long cuts, like a gash, as if something with long claws had slashed it. The wound was bloody and recent, just beginning to scab over.

"What cuts a deer like that?" Chief Lavoie growled as he bent down to inspect the buck.

Otto says nothing. He just looks up at the Chief, knowing it's time for the man to hear the truth.

"We all need to talk," Otto says, almost stammering, pushing each word out one by one. "Something really bad is happening in Berlin. And your brother is causing it."

· · · • • • • • ● • • • • • • · · ·

It takes quite a bit of coaxing, but Otto gets Marie and Chief Lavoie to come to his house on the edge of the forest.

Marie insists on bringing her friend Martha, and Otto agrees, then calls Clementine to make sure she will be there too. He knows it isn't safe to have this conversation at the police station or anywhere else. He's learned that much from his past in Robin. They have to handle this on their own. Otherwise, things could get very messy, very quickly.

Otto's house is considered a mansion by Berlin standards. The sprawling home sits like a jewel against the dark treeline of Jericho Mountain. Its renovated exterior gleams in stark contrast to the weathered apartment complexes and aging colonials that make up the rest of the small mountain community.

Otto sits at the head of the long dining room table in the kitchen, which has a floor-to-ceiling window overlooking the forest.

Also seated at the table are Marie, Martha, Chief Lavoie, Clementine, and Otto's mother, Bernice. After what happened in the forest, Bernice insisted on being involved. Lying at their feet, listening in, are Bernice's prize Irish wolfhounds, their ears perked just enough to make one wonder if they truly understand what's being said.

Chief Lavoie is the most irritated of the group. His face is flushed red, likely due to anger, though possibly from the stiff old-fashioned Bernice made sure everyone at the table had in hand for this important discussion.

The Chief remains surprisingly quiet during the first part of the conversation. Otto does his best to lead the group, as a mayor should, careful not to jump to conclusions too quickly.

"So, you're telling me that my brother is alive and my mother is a witch?" Chief Lavoie growls.

It's Marie who answers. She nods and looks down at her whiskey. "Yes."

Otto watches Clementine's reaction from across the table. Her dark eyes widen and she begins to let out a small laugh. "Witches?"

"And so am I," chimes in Martha.

Chief Lavoie nods and swallows hard as he folds his arms across his chest. "And I'm supposed to believe that you... turned him into a giant rabbit?"

"And banished him to the forest," Martha adds.

"You can't be serious," Chief Lavoie says. His voice booms across the room so loudly that it makes the hair on Otto's arms stand up. Otto has seen Chief Lavoie get loud in the past, but never at his own mother.

"It was the only way," Marie says as tears well in her blue eyes.

"Only way to what?" Chief Lavoie presses.

"To keep him from hurting anyone else. Or going to jail," Marie cries. Her eyes are bloodshot and watery, and Otto feels a small pang in his chest. This is probably her worst birthday ever.

Chief Lavoie grips his whiskey glass, his face deepening in colour.

"My brother was... is... a sick, twisted fuck. But to turn him into a rabbit and banish him to the forest? To what end? I don't understand, I..."

"I'm struggling with this too," Clementine says. "Why would you turn your son into a monster if he was already a demon?"

Marie swallows hard. "The spell... it wasn't supposed to be this way. If you had been there, you would understand. We had to—"

Across the table, Otto's mother, Bernice, clears her throat. Her voice is calm and steady.

"I think you should tell him, Marie."

Otto's head snaps toward her. *Tell them what?*

With trembling hands, Marie tucks her hair behind her ears. She glances at Martha, almost as if seeking permission to speak. She looks embarrassed that Bernice knows the secret they have worked so hard to bury.

"You know?" Marie asks, her voice barely above a whisper.

"Know what?" Chief Lavoie barks.

"Shhh." Otto cuts him off and turns to Bernice. "Mom?"

Bernice folds her hands on the table. "If I can be honest, it's been a very long time since I even heard this story. But I remember it now. When you were younger, Otto, maybe in first or second grade, there was a girl in your class named Phoebe." She glances at Marie, as if asking for permission to continue.

Marie nods while wiping the tears from her eyes. "Please, go on. I don't want to talk about it."

Bernice nods and continues. "Nolan, you were a bit older. Probably fifth or sixth grade. John was in eleventh or twelfth, right, Marie?"

Marie nods again as Martha begins to console her.

"And John and Phoebe... they formed a very inappropriate relationship," Bernice says, her voice trailing off. "I don't know all the details, but the town talked about it a lot. Phoebe's parents weren't around, and back then Berlin only had one K through twelve school. They used the same bus stop and developed a friendship that crossed a line."

Otto feels his face grow hot, anger rising in his chest. He grips his glass so tightly that his hands start to sweat.

"Ma, are you trying to say John is a pedophile?"

Marie lets out a cry from across the table and buries her head in her hands.

"He didn't... he's not a..."

She breaks down, crying uncontrollably, as Martha rubs her back.

"May I finish the story?" Martha asks gently.

Bernice nods and settles back in her seat.

Martha turns to Chief Lavoie, who sits with his arms folded across his chest. His face is cherry red, like he's about to blow a gasket.

"Your mother and I stopped this before anything could happen. At least, we think we did. When your mother found out what was going on, she confronted John."

"And?" Chief Lavoie growls.

"And he admitted to taking a liking to the girl in a way that was deeply... unwell. And when your mother confronted him about it, he became belligerent. Even as a teenager, John was twice her size. And he hit her."

Silence falls over the room. Otto looks across at Clementine, who sits anxiously, eyes fixed on her hands. Her long braids drape over her shoulders, and every few minutes she shakes her head in disgust as she listens to Martha.

As Otto listens, his mind begins to drift. He can't stop thinking about last night. This creature in the woods might be a pedophile? And he had been talking to Lily all this time?

Something inside Otto begins to shift. Yesterday, he feared the Fool. He saw the threat as a mayor, focused on protecting his community. But now, as Martha reveals more of John's past, Otto sees it through the eyes of a father. A father who wants revenge, no matter how gruesome it may be.

Otto has never considered himself a violent man. Yes, there have been moments when he had to use force to defend himself or the people he loves. But now, as he sits at the table, something else rises in him. Something furious. Something that will stop at nothing to ensure that John, the Fool, or whatever he is, never hurts anyone or anything again.

CHAPTER 6

Help

"When Marie confronted John about Phoebe, he showed no remorse. No understanding that the situation was inappropriate. It was like he had no moral compass at all," Martha says, holding her whiskey glass in one hand and Marie's trembling hand in the other. "When Marie told me what happened, she asked for my advice, and I told her about the Fool spell."

Across the room, Otto watches Clementine shift in her seat. He wants so badly to know what she's thinking. Clementine is a tried-and-true FBI agent. A government grunt. Of course, she's talented, beautiful, and brilliant, but Otto can't help wondering how she's processing all this talk about magic.

When he first learned about magic, he had been just as resistant as anyone else might be. Otto had always considered himself grounded, practical. But the first time he looked evil in the eyes, the first time he realized how little he truly understood about the world, something shifted. He began to open his mind to everything strange and unexplainable.

Would Clementine experience something similar?

"It was the spell or prison," Martha says, her voice firm. "This wasn't the only problem we had with John by then. He had a particular interest in inflicting pain on others."

Chief Lavoie exhales. "That's the understatement of the year."

"So we performed the spell, but something went wrong," Martha continues. "To this day, I don't know what we messed up, but his transformation didn't go as planned."

"And what exactly is that?" Clementine asks, raising her eyebrows. Otto can tell she's having a hard time taking it all in.

"Fools," Martha continues, "aren't supposed to talk. They're meant to be mute, like a rabbit. But something was different about John. It was like he preserved part of his humanity... and not the good part."

"And all these years, nothing else has happened until now?" Clementine asks, shaking her head. "I just have a hard time believing that."

Marie looks up from her lap and meets Clementine's gaze across the table. She pulls her hand away from Martha's and wipes the tears from her eyes.

"It's my fault. Everything that's happening now... it's because of me."

"Oh, Marie," Martha says gently.

"No, it is. For all these years, I visited him every night. Brought him food. He was always hungry. He would hunt in the woods, but it never seemed to be enough. John had an intense craving for meat. There were only two times in all these years that I forgot to go. The first time, he lashed out at me. The second time... he must have been so angry that he never came back."

Silence fills the room. Otto watches the others, gauging their reactions. He swallows hard, reminding himself that he has to take control. He is the mayor. It's his job to fix this. And now, it's his job to get revenge, for Lily and for Sandy.

"Marie, we need you to reverse the spell," Otto says. "We also need you to take us to the tunnels where John is hiding. Did he ever tell you about them?"

Marie nods. "Yes. He said they were on Jericho Mountain. At least, that's what he told me."

"Will you help us?" Otto asks.

Marie bites her bottom lip. "I... I..."

Chief Lavoie slams his hands on the table, rattling everyone's whiskey glasses. His face has shifted from tomato red to an almost purplish hue.

"Ma, for the love of God. You have to stop covering for John. He is messed up in the head, and he needs to be punished."

"He's still your brother," Marie says, her voice trembling. "You don't know if he took that girl. Maybe it's a misunderstanding—"

"He admitted it," Clementine cuts in. "In the woods. He almost took another girl with him. I've worked in law enforcement my whole life. I've never believed in witches or any of this stuff you're all talking about tonight. But when I saw that... creature... in the woods, when I shot a dozen bullets into it and it didn't even move, I knew then I wasn't dealing with something normal. We have to stop him. If we don't, this is only going to get worse. And I can't let that happen. I'll call the authorities."

Otto's chest tightens at the thought of involving the federal government. It would only complicate things, if they even believed their wild story in the first place.

"Don't say that, Clementine. We don't need to involve more people than necessary. We can handle this ourselves."

"I agree," Chief Lavoie growls. "No feds. Period."

Clementine laughs. "What if this doesn't work? What if your mother refuses to reverse the spell or hex, or whatever you call it? What if Sandy is still alive, and we have the chance to save her, but we don't have any backup because this creature is stronger than everyone at this table combined? Then what?

What if she dies, not because of John, but because we were unprepared?"

Silence settles over the room.

"Nolan and I are the only ones here who know how to properly handle a gun or have any experience finding a missing person," Clementine says. Her voice rises slightly, and her dark eyes glimmer beneath the low light of the chandelier.

Otto's stomach churns. He knows she has a point. What if they really are putting Sandy in even greater danger by refusing help?

But then again, he also knows exactly what happens when governments and law enforcement get involved in the strange, the unexplained, or the occult. Nothing good. Every story he ever heard from Dr. Brighton and her research in demonology made one thing crystal clear: never involve politicians, the government, or the cops. More often than not, they find a way to make *you* the bad guy.

Sure, Otto himself is a politician.

And Clementine and Chief Lavoie are both cops.

But Otto likes to think they're the exception. This situation is personal. They're too close to the matter to be lumped in with the rest.

He opens his mouth to speak, but the doorbell cuts him off.

"Are you expecting anyone?" Bernice asks.

Otto shakes his head as he rises from the table. "I'll be right back," he says, while the others continue their conversation. As he walks toward the door, he can still hear Clementine and Chief Lavoie passionately debating their sides.

He moves down the long hallway toward the front of the house.

Who would be here this late?

It's almost midnight, and Otto's mother always said nothing good happens after midnight. She was mostly right. But when Otto looks through the peephole, he finds himself surprised.

A smile breaks across his face, and he opens the door with enthusiasm.

Standing on the doorstep is Dr. Beatrix Brighton. She's bundled in a long orange peacoat, her hands tucked into her pockets. Dark curls, touched with grey, frame her sharp green eyes, the eyes of someone who has stared down more than one evil and somehow lived to tell the tale.

"Dr. Brighton!" Otto says.

The past few days have been filled with darkness, and a small part of him can't help but feel relieved. There's a chance he won't have to go through this alone. Someone is here who understands him, or at least understands a part of him that no one else could.

Dr. Brighton smiles, then glances behind her at the long, winding dirt driveway leading up to Otto's house. Thick pine trees line both sides, fading into a dark thicket.

"You really live out there," she says with a laugh. "I drove all the way up here thinking, there must be a nice little town at the end of this road. Why else would Otto live so far north? But this town... it's even more rural than Robin, isn't it?"

Otto nods and grips the doorframe. "It is. It really is. But it's home."

Dr. Brighton nods in return. "I understand that."

For a moment, silence settles between them. Then Dr. Brighton gently breaks it.

"I'm old, you know that. I don't think I'll be much help. But after you visited me, I couldn't just sit at home wondering what you were getting yourself into. I couldn't do it. It was going to drive me mad. It was so good to see you again, and I was happy to see you doing well. I just thought, maybe, just maybe, something I do might still be useful. These days, I have nothing to lose. I—"

Otto steps forward and pulls her into a hug.

"I'm so happy you're here," he says.

CHAPTER 7

Friends

Lily is irritated. She hates it when her father has friends over. All they do is yell, laugh, and drink until the early hours of the morning. How is a girl supposed to sleep when all she hears is other people having fun? Especially when that girl is incredibly grounded. It feels like her father and grandmother are flaunting their freedom in her face:

See? If you only behaved, you could be having a nice time with us!

By now, Lily has tried everything to fall asleep. She's counted the little glowing stick-on stars on her ceiling. She's counted backwards from 100. At one point, she even walked over to her bookshelf and pulled down what she believed was the most boring book she owned. Maybe it's because she still doesn't know what all the words mean, but every other time Lily tried to read *Encyclopedia Brown*, it put her right to sleep.

But not tonight.

After hours of trying, Lily finally accepts that she's not going to fall asleep. She eases herself out of bed and walks over to the large window in her bedroom. It's the same window she climbed out of last night when she wandered into the forest looking for Sandy. At the foot of the window sits a little bench, perfect for reading and lounging in the glow of the sun. It's night now, so the moon will do just fine.

Lily sits on the bench and pulls her knees up to her chest as she looks out the window. Her room has a clear view of the dark forest that stretches all the way to the foot of Jericho Mountain.

Just looking at the forest makes her stomach turn.

Part of her is mad at herself.

How could she have been so silly to think that BFF would help her find Sandy? How could she have been so naive? She's only a girl, after all, but even a girl can recognize concerning behavior... and know it might not be the best idea to wander into the woods alone looking for someone like that.

Sometimes, when BFF sat at the edge of the forest and talked to her, he scared her. He could be oddly possessive.

One afternoon, Lily had been sitting near the trees, telling him about what happened at school that day.

"I got written up because Sandy and I were talking during quiet time," she said, eyes downcast as she stared at the grass.

When she talked to BFF, she often looked down at the green blades and plucked them from the ground, twiddling them between her fingers. It soothed her in a strange way. It made Lily feel like she had some small control in a world that was often unkind to her.

"I don't like that Sandy got you in trouble," BFF said from the bushes. Per their typical arrangement, BFF was hidden in the bushes, completely out of Lily's line of sight. "I don't think you should be hanging out with her. She's a bad influence on you, and she's going to get you into trouble."

Lily shook her head. "No. It's my fault. I wanted to talk to Sandy about the book I just read, and I couldn't help myself."

A low growl emanated from the woods, making the hairs on Lily's arms stand up stick straight. It sounded like a growl a bear would make, not a boy, or a man, or whatever she thought BFF was at the time.

"Lily, every time you tell me a story where you get into trouble at school, Sandy is there," BFF said.

Lily shrugged her shoulders. "I guess. But isn't that what happens when someone is your best friend? You get in trouble together."

BFF didn't reply. They just sat in silence.

Though Lily was young, she certainly wasn't stupid. And it was at that point she realized that BFF may not have been Sandy's biggest fan.

• • • • • • • ● • • • • • • • • •

As Lily sits in her window, looking out into the dark forest, she decides to play another game to try and make herself fall asleep. As the adults downstairs seem to grow louder and louder, she does her best to distract herself by counting the pine trees. Not all the trees, just the pine trees.

In their backyard, there are quite a few different types of trees: birch trees, maple trees, and of course, the tall emerald pine trees that loom the highest in the forest.

One...

Two...

Three...

Lily scans the yard, counting one by one until she reaches seventeen pine trees.

And that's when she sees it, the thing that makes her blood run cold.

Nestled between pine tree number eighteen and pine tree number nineteen are a few bushes. Sticking out from the bushes are two big white rabbit ears that look... wrong. They're too large for a normal rabbit, battered and worn. One is stained with blood, and a chunk is missing from the left ear.

Lily blinks and looks again, hoping that when she opens her eyes, the strange ears will be gone.

But they aren't. They're still there, waiting. Tempting her.

The ears twitch once, as if sensing her gaze, and Lily realizes with growing dread that BFF may have been watching far longer than she had been looking back.

In that moment, Lily wishes more than anything that she weren't a girl. She wishes she were a grown-up, like her father or Clementine. Because if she were a grown-up like them, she wouldn't be sitting around the dining room, drinking and talking loudly. She would run into the woods after the creature and bring Sandy home.

But as she presses her face closer to the cold glass, a terrible thought creeps into her mind.

What if Sandy is already past saving?

What if those bloodstained ears are all that remain of her best friend's last moments?

CHAPTER 8

Plans

"This is Dr. Brighton," Otto says as he stands at the head of the table, with Dr. Brighton beside him. "She's a demonologist. World renowned. And she's here to help us."

Across the table, Bernice's eyes light up. "*You're* Dr. Brighton?"

Over the years, Otto had told his mother everything that happened at Robin State College. And though they had never met, he knew his mother had always admired what Dr. Brighton had done for her son.

Dr. Brighton nods as Bernice rises from her chair. She walks around the table and takes Dr. Brighton's hands.

"Thank you. Thank you so much for everything," Bernice says.

Dr. Brighton smiles and gives a small shrug. "You have an amazing son," she says. "You raised him very well. And I'm happy to help however I can. Maybe it's not much, but whatever I *can* do, I'm happy to offer."

"A demonologist?" Clementine laughs. "So we can bring more people into this, as long as they aren't law enforcement?"

Dr. Brighton laughs too and gently releases Bernice's hands. "I know I'm probably not what you expected when it comes to asking for help, but hopefully I can be of some value."

"Without Dr. Brighton, we'd still be trying to figure out what we're dealing with," Otto adds. "We're lucky to have her here."

Clementine swallows hard and shifts in her seat.

Otto takes a seat at the head of the table, and Dr. Brighton sits beside him. She places her hands on the table, and Bernice offers to make her a drink. As the room shifts into quiet conversation, Otto can't help but glance at Dr. Brighton's hands resting in front of her. They're worn and wrinkled, adorned with silver rings set with small jewels.

Across her right palm is a thick, pink scar, jagged, as if it had been carved with a dull bread knife.

Otto wonders what his old professor might have gotten herself into. Whatever it was, it couldn't have been good.

Should he ask her what happened?

For some reason, he can't take his eyes off the scar. It sits there like a thought he can't push out of his mind.

Bernice returns with a whiskey glass and sets it in front of Dr. Brighton. She reaches for it quickly and takes a sip.

Just as Otto opens his mouth to ask her about the scar, he's interrupted by the sound of someone running down the stairwell beside the living room. The steps are quick and soft, echoing through the dining room.

Everyone goes quiet and turns to look toward the far edge of the room that borders the hallway.

Suddenly, Lily appears in the doorway. Her bright red hair is frazzled, and her pale blue eyes are bloodshot and tired. She holds her bandaged arm close to her chest. The white gauze is streaked with brown-tinted blood, a grim reminder of where the Fool had grabbed her with his long, sharp talons the night before.

Dr. Brighton turns to Otto with a smile. "Is that Lily?"

Otto nods, his stomach tightening. Lily should be asleep, and she's usually a sound sleeper. Something is very wrong.

"She looks just like her," Dr. Brighton says. "Remarkable."

"Is everything okay, Bean?" Otto asks as he rises from the table.

The whole room is watching Lily now, hanging on her silence, waiting for her to speak.

Lily shakes her head.

Otto walks toward her and bends down to her level, meeting her bright blue eyes. She looks like she's been crying.

He rests a gentle hand on her shoulder.

"What's going on, Lily?"

Lily takes a deep breath. "Why isn't anyone trying to save Sandy?" Her voice catches, and then she bursts into tears. "You're all sitting here. You're just sitting here when she's in danger."

Otto pulls her into a hug, rubbing her back softly. "We are, Lily. We *are* trying to save Sandy. That's why everyone is here. Do you understand?"

He pulls back to meet her teary gaze as she sniffles. "Every single one of us here is working tirelessly to bring Sandy home."

Lily nods and wipes her cheeks. "But... you should be out in the forest. Looking for her."

Otto nods. "We are going to. First thing in the morning, we'll head out and find her."

"But... but BFF is outside *now*," Lily says, her voice rising.

Otto's chest tightens. He feels the weight of the room as everyone turns to look at Lily.

"You can get him now! You can—"

Otto gently takes her hands. "What do you mean he's outside now?"

Lily's voice begins to tremble as she lowers it to a near whisper. "He's been standing by the tree for the past hour. Just... watching the house. I thought he would go away, but he didn't. At first, he was hiding in the bushes, and I watched from my window. But then he stood up. He looks... sick. He waved to me. And that's when I came down here."

Otto's blood runs cold. "Show me."

The entire room rises from the table. Chief Lavoie, Marie, Martha, Dr. Brighton, Clementine, and Bernice all follow Otto and Lily to the large floor-to-ceiling windows that overlook the property and face the forest.

At first, Otto sees nothing but darkness. Then his eyes adjust, and he spots it.

A tall, white figure stands perfectly still at the edge of the forest, right where the backyard grass meets the tree line. It's partially hidden in the bushes, which rise to its waist. Its thick, long, muscular torso stretches out of the brush.

Otto begins to sweat. Seeing it again under the moonlight, it's uglier than he remembered. Its fur is matted, pressed down with a brownish-red substance that could be blood, dirt, or worse. Its long ears are tattered and torn, as if pieces have been ripped away.

"Fuck," Clementine breathes. "You know... I still can't believe this is happening."

Otto swallows hard as he watches the massive creature, easily eight feet tall, with the same warped proportions he saw the night before. Legs too long. Arms too long. Ears too long. A body too muscular for a man, and far too monstrous for any kind of rabbit.

As they watch, it begins pacing back and forth along the forest's edge like a caged wolf. It looks angry. Huffing and puffing, as if it wants nothing more than to break free and tear them apart, one by one.

"Lily, did the Fool do that to you?" Dr. Brighton asks, nodding toward Lily's bandages.

Lily nods.

Dr. Brighton folds her arms. "She's been marked. That's why he's here. When a Fool marks its prey—"

"Prey?" Lily asks, her eyes widening.

Dr. Brighton brings a hand to her mouth, startled. "I'm sorry. I forget you're a child. Um... anyway. When the Fool marks someone, and they can't be near that person, they get obsessive. Angry."

Otto hears Marie begin to sob behind him, overcome with guilt.

"I'm so sorry, Mayor Finch. I had no idea."

As much as Marie moans and wails and laments, Otto can barely focus on her. Quite simply, he doesn't care. What's done is done, and all he can think about now is running into the woods, killing that demon, and bringing Sandy home.

He turns his attention back to the forest and the creature, which continues pacing back and forth like a dog trapped behind an invisible electric fence.

Then suddenly, it stops. It turns to face the window directly.

Otto's chest tightens. The yellow eyes of the Fool, of John, stare straight at him. Even through the thick glass, Otto can feel the evil radiating off the creature. Its gaze is wild and hungry, and when Otto looks at its mouth, he sees streaks of brown staining its chin.

Very slowly, the creature raises one clawed hand and waves at the house. The gesture is almost cheerful, like a neighbor saying hello. Then it opens its mouth into a sinister grin, revealing white buck teeth that resemble vampire fangs more than the teeth of any rabbit.

"He wants me to come outside, doesn't he?" Lily whispers.

Otto grabs her shoulders and shakes his head. "No, Lily. He doesn't. He—"

"We have to go out there. Now," Chief Lavoie says, cutting through the silence.

"Are you mad?" Bernice snaps, looking up at him. She's about a foot shorter than Chief Lavoie, but that's never stopped her from challenging anyone before. If there's one thing Otto knows about his mother, it's that she doesn't back down.

Dr. Brighton places a gentle hand on Bernice's arm. "He's right, Mrs. Finch. We might not get this chance again. If the Fool, John, is who he claims to be, he might just lead us straight to the girl."

Otto swallows hard. The idea of venturing into the woods this late isn't lost on him. But the longer they wait, the less likely they are to find Sandy alive.

"If there's one thing I know about my sick excuse for a brother," Chief Lavoie growls, "it's that he likes to show off his work. Even when we were kids. Every time he did something gross or evil, he'd lead you straight to it. He can't help himself."

Otto turns back to the window and watches the Fool. It stands motionless, smiling faintly, its body swaying slightly as if in a trance. Then, slowly, it turns and walks into the forest, unhurried, like it has all the time in the world.

"Okay," Otto says, taking a deep breath. "We'll follow him."

CHAPTER 9

Righting Wrongs

O nce the Fool disappears into the forest, Otto urges the group to move quickly. Chief Lavoie agrees to lead them into the woods, joined by a reluctant Clementine, who makes it clear, more than once, that she would much prefer to wait until they had backup before heading into the dark New Hampshire forest to chase an evil creature created by two witches.

But she's quickly and unanimously overruled.

No one wants to get anyone else involved.

Otto knows Chief Lavoie is worried about his job. Otto himself is worried about his reputation. Dr. Brighton clearly knows better than to trust the authorities. And poor Marie and Martha are terrified of being found out as witches.

"All we need to do is find the tunnels, find Sandy, and then... reverse the spell," Otto says, as the group buzzes around the room, preparing to head out into the forest. At this point, he's really trying to convince Marie. Everyone else is already on board.

Chief Lavoie has his gun.

Clementine has hers.

Otto has distributed the few hunting rifles he owns to Dr. Brighton and Bernice.

Bernice had agreed to stay behind and watch Lily, but Otto made sure she was armed, just in case something strange happened.

Marie is the only one dragging her feet, unable to make a decision. Martha, on the other hand, had made her stance crystal clear. She refused to join them. She called John "sadistic," and "twisted," and she called the group foolish for even trying.

So it all fell on Marie. Without her help, even if they were lucky enough to find Sandy, it was likely that John would continue his reign of terror anyway.

"I... I don't even know if I remember the spell," Marie says, sitting at the table with her arms folded.

Dr. Brighton, uncomfortably holding a small rifle, reaches into her pocket, pulls out a piece of paper, and slaps it down on the table. The rings on her fingers strike the surface with a sharp crack as she slides the paper toward Marie.

"It's right here," Dr. Brighton says. "I just need you to read it backward. Then this will all be over."

Marie sighs and nods. She reaches for the paper and studies it quietly.

"And what happens when he's human again? Isn't that dangerous? A spell reversal could kill him."

Otto, who had been silently watching the exchange, wanted to say that once John was human again, he would shoot him between the eyes and make sure that scum never hurt another child. But he doesn't say that. Instead, he steps closer to Marie, bends to her level, and gently places a hand on her arm. He looks into her silvery-blue eyes, still red from crying.

"Marie, he hurt a little girl," Otto says.

Marie swallows hard. "You... you don't know that. She could be fi—"

"No, Marie," Otto says firmly. He shakes his head and points to Lily, who is sitting with Bernice in the corner of the room. "He hurt my daughter. He coaxed her into the woods. He stalked her for months. And then he hurt her. Took his long claws and drove them so deep into her arm that her bones almost broke. I don't know what he did to Sandy, but if it's anything like what he did to my daughter, he deserves to be in prison for a very long time."

Tears begin to well in Marie's eyes again. "I'm sorry. I'm so sorry."

Dr. Brighton places her free hand on Marie's shoulder. "The best way you can fix this is by helping us end it once and for all."

Marie nods. "But I'm an old woman. I don't know how far I'll make it into the woods with you all."

"I'm an old woman too," Dr. Brighton replies. "And if I can do it, you can do it."

Marie shakes her head. "I just turned eighty."

Dr. Brighton shrugs. "Age is a number. We will do this together," she says, gently squeezing her shoulder.

"Plus," Otto adds, "if John still cares about you and loves you, you can reason with him. You're our only hope at saving Sandy."

Dr. Brighton nods. "This is how you right your wrongs."

CHAPTER 10

Teeth

As Dr. Brighton stands at the edge of the woods beside Otto, Clementine, Chief Lavoie, and Marie, she can't help but let out a small laugh. Is she really going to do this? Are they really about to chase the Fool into the woods? In all her years as a demonologist, she had never actually encountered a Fool in real life. The first time she saw one was just an hour ago, looking out Otto's window. And she still couldn't believe how ugly the creature was in person.

They were rarely mentioned in her studies, and some naive part of her had assumed it would look like a giant rabbit. Maybe something like the Rodents of Unusual Size from *The Princess Bride*. But the Fool was somehow more sinister. Larger, stronger, and uglier, it looked like it had the power to crush every single one of them without even trying.

Were they fools too, heading into the woods like this?

Had she helped lead this group on a wild goose chase?

Or worse, into a trap?

She isn't sure. But as she looks down at the large scar on her right hand, she remembers. She noticed Otto eyeing it earlier. Ever since she got it, about ten years ago, it had felt like a stain on her body that she could never wash off.

She wasn't proud of it. In fact, she was mortified by it and what it meant. Every single time she looked at that fucking scar, it made her stomach turn. It symbolised everything she stood against in this world. It symbolised evil and damnation. Because she was one of the few people alive who knew exactly what it meant.

To her, it meant that no matter how much good she did in this world, no matter how hard she tried to do the right thing, no matter what, she was eternally damned. To hell.

Yes, that one.

H-E-DOUBLE HOCKEY STICKS, as the kids say.

But there was one good thing about the scar on her hand that she sometimes failed to notice. The scar, though painful to look at, made her incredibly brave, even at her age. Dr. Brighton was a few years shy of seventy now, and everything moved much slower. In theory, she should have been terrified of walking into the woods and coming face-to-face with the Fool.

But she wasn't.

And it was because of her scar.

It gave her an unearned sense of bravery that would allow her to do anything in her power to help Otto save Sandy, even if it came at her own expense.

After all, nothing mattered anymore.

In her final years on this Earth, all she could do was her best to help those who needed it most. And that is exactly what Dr. Beatrix Brighton intended to do.

· · · · · · · · ● · · · · · · · · · ·

Otto stands at the edge of the forest, a rifle slung over his back. Chief Lavoie stands beside him, gazing into the trees at the path cleared by the Fool's heavy feet. It's a straight shot into the darkness, marked by footprints that are far too long and too large.

"Well," the Chief says, "you going to lead the way, Boston?"

Otto's stomach turns. He's not much of a wilderness guy. Sure, he enjoys the occasional hike, but not at one o'clock in the morning in the middle of a deep, dark forest.

Chief Lavoie punches him in the shoulder, just a bit too hard. "I'm just pulling your leg," he says with a smirk. Then he turns back to the group. "I'll lead us in. The path is pretty narrow, so Agent Miller, why don't you bring up the rear and make sure John isn't trailing us or anything. And if you see something, say something. Any type of movement in the brush, tunnels, speak up."

The Chief steps into the woods. Otto's heart races as he follows, staring at the back of the Chief's dark blue uniform. When his foot crosses the threshold of the forest, Otto feels his breath escape him. They're in the Fool's territory now. For all they know, John could be hiding in the bushes, watching them that very second.

They move along the narrow path, weaving between brush and low branches. Every few minutes, Otto feels Dr. Brighton grab the back of his coat so she doesn't lose him through the thicket. The farther they venture into the woods, the darker it becomes.

They have flashlights, but they're turned off.

That was Chief Lavoie's idea. He didn't want John to know they were coming.

"Your eyes will adjust to the darkness," the Chief had said as they debated it back at the house. "We don't need them. The flashlights will only draw attention to us. And when we walk in the woods, we are to be as quiet as a mouse. Any heads-up gives him the advantage."

But as they walk deeper into the forest, Otto begins to think the Chief might be wrong. Their eyes aren't adjusting to the darkness. If anything, the woods seem to grow darker with each step. The canopy above thickens, blotting out even the faintest traces of moonlight that had helped guide them at the forest's edge.

When the path curves slightly to the left, Chief Lavoie stops dead in his tracks. Otto nearly crashes into him.

"That fucking sicko," the Chief mutters under his breath.

"What?" Otto asks.

Chief Lavoie doesn't answer right away. He stands frozen, shoulders rigid. Otto peers around him, and that's when he sees it... and smells it. The stench is so foul he worries he might vomit.

Hanging from the branches ahead, blocking their path like a curtain, are pelts. Dozens of them. Each one dangles from a thin strand of fishing wire, like the world's most sinister Christmas ornaments. Some are small, maybe squirrels or cats. But others are larger. Otto spots one with floppy ears and immediately thinks of the missing dog from the Facebook posts he saw weeks ago. Some of the pelts still have collars.

He closes his eyes and listens as Dr. Brighton tells Marie not to look.

"We have to walk through them," Chief Lavoie says quietly. "The path doesn't go around."

When Otto reopens his eyes, he realises the Chief is right. Both sides of the trail are lined with thick, thorny brush, too dense and too high for any of them to push through.

Behind them, Marie lets out a wail. "I told him to stop. When he was little, I told him to stop with the squirrels."

Otto feels Dr. Brighton's grip tighten on his coat. Her voice is barely a whisper as she leans in close. "You know, I felt so good about this, and now I don't anymore."

He swallows hard. If Dr. Brighton, of all people, is afraid, how can he possibly keep his composure?

Ahead, the Chief takes a deep breath and pushes forward, ducking under the first pelt, doing his best to move them aside with his hands. Otto follows, searching for some kind of bravery deep inside himself. He can feel the bodies brush against his hair and shoulders. Something wet drips onto his neck. The stench of decay and copper fills his nostrils until he's forced to breathe through his mouth.

It's Dr. Brighton who notices it first.

"Otto," she whispers, her voice tight with horror. "Look at their mouths."

When Otto glances up at the hanging carcasses, his heart nearly stops. Each skinned animal has something small and white stuffed into its gaping mouth.

They look like baby teeth.

Human teeth.

They shine like pearls in the darkness.

The group moves onward quickly, pushing through the last of the hanging bodies. Suddenly, the trees open up. Otto stumbles forward, gasping for fresh air as they emerge into a wide clearing bathed in moonlight.

The clearing is empty.

Just a wide, open space surrounded by trees.

The silence feels wrong. Otto has been in the woods plenty of times before, and he knows there should be sounds. Crickets. The rustle of small animals. Wind moving through the leaves.

But there is nothing.

It is as if every living thing in this part of the forest has simply vanished.

And that is when Otto realises the most disturbing part of all. The footprints they had been following, John's massive, elongated tracks, stop abruptly at the edge of the clearing.

It is as if he simply disappeared into thin air.

CHAPTER 11

Decisions

"This can't be right," Chief Lavoie says, staring at the Fool's massive footprints that end just at the edge of the clearing. He swallows hard and quickly draws his gun, pointing it into the wide, open space. "John!" he yells. The name echoes through the woods again and again until the sound fades into a sickening silence.

"John, you son of a bitch. I know you're here. Show yourself!"

The Chief begins to walk slowly into the clearing while Otto, Clementine, Marie, and Dr. Brighton stand on the edge, side by side. Clementine draws her gun too, glancing behind them with a glimmer of worry in her eye.

Otto isn't sure what to do, so he keeps one hand on the rifle slung over his shoulder, ready in case he needs it.

He watches as Chief Lavoie walks all the way to the center of the clearing. There, the Chief stops, bends down, and picks up a piece of paper from the ground.

"What the fuck?" he mutters, narrowing his eyes as if trying to decipher ancient hieroglyphics.

"What is it?" Otto asks.

He takes a step forward but looks back to Clementine, almost for permission. Is it okay to go look?

Clementine gives him a gentle nod, signaling that she will stay with Dr. Brighton and Marie as he heads into the clearing.

As Otto crosses the threshold of the glade and steps into the open space, he cannot shake the feeling that he is being watched. Every hair on his arms rises and prickles as anxiety creeps up his spine.

What if John is sitting somewhere at the edge of the clearing, watching and waiting for the perfect moment? What if this is a trap, and Otto is walking straight into it?

Chief Lavoie's hands are shaking by the time Otto reaches him. He peers over the Chief's shoulder to see the paper clutched in his large, red hands. It is torn and tattered, lightly damp from the early morning dew. Scribbled in black ink across the centre of the page are the following words:

> She is north
>
> I am south
>
> You are fucked

Otto swallows and watches as Chief Lavoie breathes long, heavy breaths that steam in the cold night air. Then the Chief growls and crumples up the paper.

"I'm going to kill him."

Otto nods. "Do you know which way is north?"

Chief Lavoie ignores him and just shakes his head, staring down at the crumpled paper in his fist.

"Chief," Otto says, trying to get his attention. "We need to figure out which direction—"

"I know exactly where he is," Chief Lavoie interrupts, his voice low and dangerous. "South. He's probably at my mother's house. It's directly south of here if you keep going far enough."

Otto calls back to the others. "We need to head north to find Sandy!"

Clementine jogs over, with Dr. Brighton and Marie close behind. "What's the plan?" she asks, looking between Otto and Chief Lavoie.

"We go south first," the Chief says firmly. "Catch John by surprise. He's not expecting us to come for him. He thinks we'll go straight for the girl like good little heroes. Ma will say the spell, however that works, and we'll end this once and for all."

Otto shakes his head and frowns. He can't help but think of poor little Sandy sitting alone in the tunnels, scared, hungry, hopeless. That is, if she's even alive.

"No. We get Sandy first. That's the priority."

"The priority?" Chief Lavoie's face begins to redden. "The priority is stopping that monster before he hurts someone else. We take him out while we have the element of surprise, then we get the girl."

"Nolan," Marie says quietly, "I think the Mayor is right. We should save Sandy first. She's just a child. She's probably scared."

Chief Lavoie whips around to face his mother. His face is red with anger, and beads of sweat begin to roll down his forehead.

"Of course you do. You don't even want to use the spell, do you, Ma? You'll do anything to protect that bastard. Anything. You're still protecting him. Delaying the inevitable."

"That's not—"

"I'm not stupid!" the Chief explodes. "I wasn't born yesterday. Thirty years you've been lying to me, feeding that psycho, keeping him safe while he terrorises this town. And now you want to drag your feet some more?"

Marie starts crying. "I just want to save the little girl—"

"Bullshit!" Chief Lavoie yells, his voice echoing through the clearing. "You're hoping we find some excuse not to hurt your favourite son. Well, guess what, Mom? Your son is a killer. A child predator. And I'm done pretending otherwise. If you won't help me, I'll handle this on my own."

"Chief, calm down," Clementine says, stepping forward. "You don't understand what—"

"Don't tell me to calm down!" He looks around at all of them with disgust. "You know what? Fine. Go play rescue mission. Hold hands and sing songs while that monster slips away again. But I'm not allowing it."

Chief Lavoie turns to Otto and points his thick finger in his face.

"And you. I expected better out of you, Boston. He almost took your daughter, and you want to let him slip through our fingers because you're scared of a fucking rabbit? Foolish."

The Chief shakes his head and starts walking toward the southern edge of the clearing.

"Where are you going?" Otto calls after him.

Chief Lavoie turns back, his face twisted with rage and determination. "To finish what should have been finished thirty years ago. This ends tonight, with or without you."

"Nolan, please!" Marie cries.

But her son is already disappearing into the darkness of the southern woods, leaving them standing helpless in the moonlit clearing.

CHAPTER 12

Pride

Chief Lavoie trudges through the woods with his gun raised, eyeing the bushes and searching for those sinister yellow eyes. He wants nothing more than to run into John, to tell him exactly what kind of creep he is, and then to shoot him right between the eyes with his pistol. Nolan has waited his whole life for this moment, a chance to get even with the most twisted man he's ever known. His brother.

Even though Clementine had explained earlier that bullets didn't stop John, Nolan feels like this time might be different. Maybe Clementine was too scared of such a horrific creature. Maybe her aim wasn't great. Or perhaps it had just been a fluke.

Regardless, Chief Lavoie pushes through the brush with reckless confidence. The deeper he goes, the more agitated he becomes. Unwanted memories flash through his mind.

John tackling him on the playground, beating him until his lip bled.

When Nolan was seven and his brother handed him a sandwich by the pool, he bit down and found it packed with live worms that burst between his teeth, their guts slithering across his tongue.

That time at Lake Winnipesaukee when Nolan was eight. John jumped on his shoulders and held him underwater until he thought he would die. Water filled his mouth as he struggled to hold his breath. John's harsh hands dragged him up just before he blacked out.

But worst of all, the memory that makes Nolan cringe the most, was when John was thirteen, arguing with their mother. Little Nolan had watched as Marie told John "no" one too many times. John wound up his arm and slapped his own mother across the face with a sickening crack.

It wasn't the slap that upset Nolan the most. It was his mother's tears when she realised her own son had hurt her.

The Chief feels his face grow hot the more he dwells on the past. As he walks, he becomes more certain that he made the right decision by handling this alone. Forget spells. Forget teamwork. If anyone is going to end this madness, it should be him.

After what feels like an eternity of walking south, he begins to recognise the footsteps on the ground. They appear suddenly, all pointing in the same direction, south. As if John had appeared out of nowhere and started walking, leaving behind a trail of breadcrumbs.

"I know you're out here, brother," he calls into the woods. "Come out, and we can end this once and for all. Brother to brother."

Only the silence of the forest answers him.

"Come on out," Chief Lavoie says again. "I came where you told me to."

He looks into the distance and sees his mother's house behind the edge of the trees, sitting quietly with all the lights off. No one is home.

A branch snaps behind him, and he jumps.

He whips around, finger on the trigger, but there is nothing there. Just darkness between the trees.

Shaking his head, he keeps trudging through the forest, making his way toward the edge of the woods and the same tree stump where his mother sat just last night when she told him the sickening news that his brother was still alive.

Next to the stump is the picnic basket Marie left behind in a hurry. It's still there, sitting like nothing has changed. Unopened.

Something deep in the Chief's chest pulls him toward the basket. He wants to open it so badly. What has Marie been feeding John all these years?

But as he takes a step closer, he realises a horrible smell is coming from it. Something rotten. Something that reeks of death.

He slowly eases the lid open and is met with a wave of stench that swims up through his nostrils. When he looks inside the little wicker basket, his stomach drops. Nestled inside is a grotesque collection of dead animals. A fox lies across the top, its tongue hanging out of its mouth, sharp white teeth bared. Beneath the fox are about half a dozen squirrels, some flattened by car tires, some missing eyes or tails. And at the very bottom of the basket is a dead porcupine. Its quills are relaxed, and its snout is still faintly pink.

"Roadkill," coos a voice from the bushes.

Chief Lavoie looks up so quickly he lets go of the lid, which snaps shut with a loud clap.

When he looks up, two yellow eyes are staring back at him from the bushes.

"You know how Mom likes to go on her long drives," the voice says with a little giggle. "She collects them for me. Sometimes I think she even kills them herself, Nolly. Isn't that nice? Mommy always said I was her favorite."

Now that he's face to face with the creature, every ounce of pride and bravery drains from Chief Lavoie's body. He stands frozen in front of the bushes, pale and breathless.

"The porcupines always taste the best," the voice continues, still cooing. "Sure, the quills get in the way sometimes, but they add an extra crunch. Can't get that anywhere else from anything else. It's unique. You know, Nolly, there's something so delightful about death. Freshness is... overrated. Once you leave something sitting out in the sun for a bit, exposed to the air and the earth, it just tastes richer, in a way."

Chief Lavoie opens his mouth to speak, but no words come out.

"Want me to come out, Nolly? You want to see your big brother? Give me a big old hug? It's been many years. But I've been watching you. Keeping an eye on you. When you and your goons came into the woods looking for Sandy, I thought it was sweet. You looking for that little girl."

A low laugh.

"You know, I haven't seen you get off your fat ass in ages, Nolly. You've put on a few over the years. But so have I."

As the words leave the creature's mouth, it takes a step forward, bringing its horrible face into the moonlight.

The Chief feels like he's going to faint. Every ounce of rage has drained from his body now that he sees the creature up close.

The thing that steps out of the bushes is massive, easily eight feet tall, with arms that hang down past its knees. Its white fur is matted and streaked with brown stains that could be blood or feces. Its long ears are tattered, with chunks missing, as if something had been gnawing on them.

But it's the face that makes Nolan's stomach lurch. John's human features are still there, twisted and elongated. His eyes have the same almond shape they always did, but now they glow yellow in the darkness. His mouth juts forward to make room for massive buck teeth that look more like fangs. And his long French-Canadian nose has warped into something monstrous, with thick whiskers jutting out in every direction.

"Miss me, Nolly?"

Chief Lavoie fumbles for his gun, his hands shaking as he draws it. He fires once. Twice. Three times. He empties the clip into John's chest.

The creature doesn't even flinch. Thick, dark blood oozes from the bullet holes, but John only tilts his head like a curious dog.

"That's not very nice, brother," the creature says with a smile.

The Chief swallows hard. Clementine was right. They were all right. And as he stares into his brother's bright yellow eyes, he realises that in this moment, he's nothing more than the hamster John had killed when they were kids; small, defenseless, helpless, and about to die.

Before he can open his mouth to scream, John's massive white hand lunges for his throat. Hairy fingers wrap around his neck like he's nothing but a rag doll. Then the talons come, piercing through Nolan's skin, digging deeper and deeper, crushing his windpipe until he can no longer breathe.

Nolan's last image before he dies is a memory.

Being stuck underwater.

Unable to breathe.

John holding him down, squeezing out his very last breath.

"Remember the lake, little brother?" John whispers, lifting Nolan off the ground like he weighs nothing. "Remember how the water filled your lungs?"

Nolan's feet kick uselessly in the air. Blood pours down his chest as John's claws crush his windpipe. He tries to speak, to beg, but only a wet, gurgling sound escapes.

"I let you live that day," John says, his rotten breath hot against Nolan's face. "I pulled you up. Saved you." His grip tightens. "Biggest mistake I ever made."

Nolan's vision begins to blur. His lungs burn for air that will never come.

"This time," John whispers, "big brother isn't letting go."

The last thing Nolan sees before the darkness takes him is John's yellow eyes, glowing in the moonlight. The same eyes that watched him drown all those years ago at the lake.

Only this time, there's no coming back up.

CHAPTER 13

Circles

It's only been about thirty minutes since Otto and the group parted ways with Chief Lavoie in the clearing, but with each passing moment, Otto worries they've made a grave mistake by letting him wander off alone.

Nevertheless, they keep pressing on.

Otto has taken the lead, guiding them deeper into the woods, north, or at least he hopes it's north. He's following the exact direction the Chief pointed, but Otto can't shake the feeling that they might be going in circles.

"How much longer?" Marie calls from behind him.

Otto takes a deep breath as he pushes forward along the narrow path. He wishes he knew. He wishes he had some kind of answer to give them. But in truth, he has no idea where the tunnels are. They could be hours away, or just minutes. It's nearly three o'clock in the morning, and before long, the sun will begin to rise.

"I don't know," Otto mutters. For the past fifteen minutes, the ground has sloped steadily upward, climbing toward Jericho Mountain. What if they can't make it back? Every few minutes, he glances over his shoulder to check on the others.

Dr. Brighton seems fine, walking with her head down and a steady determination.

Marie, on the other hand, is barely keeping up. The group has to stop for her every few minutes. Otto can't help but wonder, what if Marie isn't strong enough to make it all the way? What if she doesn't have the strength to make it out of the woods?

This fear is starting to feel less like a worry and more like a grim reality.

Clementine is still bringing up the rear, helping Marie over rocks and tree roots with quiet, gentle care.

But what if Marie is only slowing them down?

What if Sandy is in real danger, and every second counts?

Otto tries to push the thought out of his mind, but Marie beats him to it when she stops walking and lets out a long, weary sigh.

"Can we take a break?" Marie says. "I want to call Nolan. I want to make sure that he's okay. I want him to meet back up with us. I don't feel comfortable not knowing where he is."

The rest of the group pauses and looks at Marie. Her worried eyes appear worn and tired in the moonlight, and she places both hands on her hips like a child refusing to budge until they get what they want.

Otto nods and pulls his phone from his pocket. "Don't talk for too long. I don't want to waste the battery," he says, handing it to her.

Marie grabs the phone and quickly dials. It rings and rings. She frowns when it goes to voicemail. She hangs up and tries again, biting her bottom lip as tears begin to well in her eyes.

Otto takes a deep breath. He doesn't want to think the worst, but knowing the Fool, knowing John, the worst is quite possibly their reality. For a moment, he wishes he had tried harder to stop the Chief from leaving alone. But it would have been no use. After decades of knowing Nolan, Otto understands that once he sets his mind on something, it's best to get out of his way.

When Nolan doesn't answer the phone on the third try, Marie huffs and begins to cry.

"I'm worried. I'm worried about Nolan. We should have never let him go off into the woods alone."

Clementine places her hands gently on the older woman's shoulders and begins to rub them. "We're in the middle of nowhere. Maybe he just doesn't have service?"

Otto looks over at Dr. Brighton, who meets him with a gaze that tells him she knows exactly what he's thinking, and that she agrees. Chief Lavoie made a foolish decision by wandering off into the woods alone, and it's quite possible he's paying the price.

"I want to go back," Marie says. "Back to my house. I want to see John and Nolan. I think I can reason with them."

Her body is shaking now, arms wrapped tightly around herself as if she's trying to hug the fear away.

Otto shakes his head. "No. We can't go back now. We've come all this way. And Sandy, she's waiting for us. She's the whole reason we're out here."

Tears stream down Marie's face as she shakes her head. "No. I don't care."

Otto walks over and looks her in the eye. "Just like you're worried about your sons, Sandy's parents are worried about her too. They're terrified of what could have happened to their daughter, and they have no idea what's going on. And the fact is, all of this is partially your fault."

"Otto," Clementine says, shooting him a warning look.

"Listen, I'm just being honest," Otto replies. "We can't give up now. We have to keep going. We're close. I can feel it."

Marie shakes her head. "I'm sorry, Mr. Mayor. I have to look out for my family and my sons. I want to go back. Besides, what good am I up there to you anyway? John is to the south, just like he said. That's where I can be the most helpful."

Otto shrugs and folds his arms across his chest. "Well, I don't give a damn. We aren't going with you. So unless you want to walk through this forest on your own, you're going to help us find the tunnels, and you're going to help us reverse this stupid fucking spell."

Marie shakes her head. "I won't. I'll sit right here on the ground for all I care. I am going to find my sons, and we are going to work this out. All this talk about punishment is insane. You don't even know if... if he did anything wrong. And you want me to put his whole life in danger."

"He kidnapped a girl, Marie!" Otto yells. His voice echoes through the woods. "And he tried to take my daughter. Are you insane?"

Marie says nothing. Her lip just quivers. A mother who can't believe what her own son has done. Who would rather disassociate than face the truth.

"I'll take her back," Clementine says.

Otto's eyes widen. "No, Clementine, you can't."

Clementine swallows hard and takes a deep breath. "I'll take her back, and then I'll come find you right away. You're right, you have to get to Sandy now. But I can't, in good conscience, let her walk through the woods alone. You know I can't."

Otto takes a deep breath. He wants nothing more than to shake Marie and tell her that she's the one who caused this whole mess. But he doesn't. Instead, he turns to Dr. Brighton.

"Will you come with me? Will you keep going?"

Dr. Brighton, her green eyes worn and tired, lets out a small smile and nods. "Of course."

CHAPTER 14

Crosses

"You know, I dated a witch once," Dr. Brighton says as she trudges up the mountain behind Otto. "They are very emotional. I'm more of a rational thinker. Didn't work out. Needless to say, Marie's exit doesn't surprise me."

Otto lets out a small laugh as he leads them through the forest, though he's still angry and frustrated. How could Marie be so naive about her son? How could she be so blinded that she would rather run back to him than help an innocent young girl he may have harmed?

"I just don't understand it," he says with an exhausted sigh.

"Well, people believe what they want to believe, Otto. You should know that. And sometimes, when a mother badly wants to believe her child could never do wrong, that can be one of the most powerful delusions of all. Not to mention, the reversal spell is quite dangerous. It really could kill him."

"Really?" Otto asks.

Dr. Brighton nods. "Any spell reversal is dangerous. These things, spells, hexes, are not to be taken lightly. That's why I don't mess with them. Unfortunately, there are many people in this world who think the macabre is all fun and games. But there are serious consequences to magic, even when it's done for the right reasons."

Otto nods and looks at the ground, watching his shoes crunch the twigs and leaves beneath him.

"What do you think the odds are that Nolan is dead?"

Silence settles behind him.

Dr. Brighton takes a deep breath and lets out a nervous laugh. "If I were a betting woman, which I am occasionally... well, I'm not much of a sports fan, but I do bet on the Patriots every so often. Anyway, let's just say it's like 2017 and the Patriots are in the Super Bowl."

Otto narrows his eyes. He doesn't know football that well, but he remembers how successful the Tom Brady era was for the Patriots. It was a huge deal in Berlin. The whole town came together. There were Super Bowl parties everywhere. It was the only thing happening in February, during the dead of winter.

"And?" he asks.

"I would bet a pretty substantial amount of money that the Patriots would win."

Otto swallows hard and continues trudging forward. He doesn't want to ask for any more clarification. He simply assumes there's a very high likelihood that Chief Lavoie is dead, and that Marie and Clementine may be walking into the exact same trap.

But surely Marie would protect Clementine, wouldn't she?

Surely, she would reverse the spell if John tried to harm her?

Unfortunately, Otto doesn't really know. And he doesn't want to think about it any longer.

After that, Otto doesn't have much to say. Maybe he's tired, or perhaps he has simply resigned himself to the fact that Dr. Brighton is right. Marie is delusional, and Chief Lavoie is probably dead. But he doesn't feel like talking about it anymore. He would rather just keep trudging on in uncomfortable silence.

Which he does, until, after about twenty minutes of walking north, Dr. Brighton notices a change in the forest.

"Do you smell that?" she asks.

Otto pauses and looks up into the trees. The night is slowly beginning to transform into dawn, and the moonlight no longer guides them. Only the faint, gradual fading of darkness remains.

Otto takes a deep breath, and he smells it too. A faint stench. Something rotting.

"I smell it," he says.

Dr. Brighton nods and looks into the distance. "I think we should follow it."

"The smell?" Otto asks.

She nods again and begins pulling her long hair back into a bun, as if to say, *this is the moment things get even more serious.*

With one hand on his rifle, Otto nods and starts walking, doing his best to follow the scent. As they make their way through the woods, the smell grows stronger and more distinct until they reach the edge of a clearing. It isn't the same one from earlier that morning. This clearing sits high up on the edge of the mountain, like a small ledge carved into the hillside.

And that's when Otto sees the path.

The entire clearing is filled with crosses. Hundreds of them. Wooden stakes driven into the ground in neat rows, a perverted cemetery. Each cross holds a rotting creature, a twisted concoction from John's mind. Two different bodies fused together in grotesque abomination, like John himself, only worse.

The decomposing bodies are stretched out in rancid crucifixions. The crosses are packed so tightly together that there's barely enough room for Otto or Dr. Brighton to walk between them. The flood of crosses forms a narrow, winding path that leads to a dark cave opening in the mountainside, the tunnels.

Otto's mind reels as he tries to process what he's seeing. This isn't recent work. Some of the crosses are decades old, their occupants reduced to nothing but bleached bone and matted fur clinging to skeletal frames. Thirty years of twisted artistry stretch before them.

How many nights did John spend out here, hammering stakes into the earth, crucifying his creations under the stars?

Did Marie know?

Did she know her son had been out in the wilderness, decapitating raccoons and rats, fusing their heads and limbs together in some deranged patchwork?

Otto's stomach lurches as he steps deeper into the clearing, taking in the full scope of John's grotesque work. Raccoons with swan wings. Cats with rooster heads. Dogs stitched with bat wings. Squirrels grafted with chicken feet. Fox bodies topped with duck skulls.

The combinations are endless, and horrifying. Each more putrid than the last.

And the stench. It hits him like a wall. It's the smell of a meat locker that has been unplugged for weeks, everything inside left to rot.

The older creatures have been worn down to bone. Their gaping eye sockets are hollow, while the fresher ones still drip with decay. Maggots cover the ground, writhing like white snow over the green grass. Flies buzz in thick clouds, hovering above the freshly butchered creatures.

"Jesus Christ," Dr. Brighton whispers, pulling her coat over her nose. "This is worse than I thought."

Otto swallows hard. "Why... why do you say that?"

"Because this isn't just a Fool, Otto," Dr. Brighton says as they weave between the crosses. "This is a sick fuck. How long has this been going on?"

"Decades," Otto manages, his voice hoarse. He thinks about Lily playing in their backyard, so close to this monument of madness. What if she had wandered up here instead of just to the forest's edge? What if John had brought her here before Otto realized what was happening?

His own daughter was inches away from this filth, and he had no idea.

"This is methodical," Dr. Brighton observes, her academic mind still functioning in the midst of horror. "Look at the arrangement. He's organized them by type, by age. This isn't random violence, Otto. This is obsession. Compulsion taken to its absolute extreme."

Otto looks around him.

She's right.

John had arranged all the cats' bodies in one corner, the raccoons in another, then the foxes, and even what looked like a small pony. A deer, maybe? It's hard for him to decipher some of the mutilated creatures.

They pick their way carefully down the narrow path, trying not to step on the fallen chunks of flesh and bone that litter the ground. Otto tries to breathe through his mouth, but he can taste death in the air. It's unavoidable.

"We're in his territory now," Dr. Brighton says, her voice barely a whisper. "This is where he feels strongest, most comfortable. And if Sandy is down in those tunnels, he's going to do everything he can to protect what's his. We're not just rescuing a little girl, Otto. We're stealing prey from a predator. John is an animal. You cannot think of him as human. We are far past that."

If John did this to all these creatures, then what the hell did he do to Sandy? What was he going to do to Lily?

Otto can't think about it. He just stands there, breathless.

Near the tunnel entrance, he spots a crude workstation set up between the crosses. A tree stump serves as a table, its surface black with dried blood. Scattered across it are tools, a rusty axe, a claw hammer, a red rubber mallet stained brown, several knives of different sizes, and a blood-crusted hatchet.

They walk toward the workstation as Otto stares at the tools, feeling something shift inside him. This is where John dismembered his victims. Where he sawed off limbs and heads. Where he planned each grotesque abomination. Sandy could be in that tunnel right now, and these might be the very tools John plans to use on her.

Dr. Brighton eyes the tools and reaches for the hatchet. The handle is sticky with old blood, but she grips it firmly.

"For good measure," she says, testing its weight.

Beyond the workstation, the tunnel mouth opens wide. The path of crosses leads directly to its edge, creating a funnel that channels everything in the clearing toward John's lair.

As Otto looks into the darkness of the tunnel, he realises they are about to descend into the very heart of thirty years of madness, and he has never been more terrified in his life.

CHAPTER 15

Down The Rabbit Hole

Dr. Brighton stares into the gaping mouth of the tunnel as she stands by Otto's side. The smell of rotting decay stings her nostrils. To their left lies the body of a badger, its arms spread wide, pinned to a cross. Its head is that of a pig. The eyes are wide open, and she can't shake the feeling that all of these rotting, melded creatures are watching their every move.

"You know, you don't have to come down there with me," Otto says.

Dr. Brighton lets out a small laugh, the loudest laugh someone can manage when surrounded by death. "And what? Stay up here with all these things? I think I'll pass."

Otto nods and pulls out his phone. "I'm going to send my location to Clementine so she can find us later."

Dr. Brighton nods, though she knows full well there's no chance Otto has service this far up the mountain. She watches him fiddle with his phone, a frown forming on his face.

She reaches out and grabs his anxious, trembling hand, meeting his dark brown eyes. They look bloodshot and weary behind his glasses.

"We have to do this on our own, Otto. It will be okay."

He doesn't look convinced. "But what if he follows us down there and we get trapped? Then what? No one will be able to find us."

She grips his hand tighter. "If anything happens down there, I want you to promise me one thing, Otto. If you get the chance to leave with the girl, leave. Do not wait for me. Do not let me slow you down. You grab that girl and you get the hell out of there. I can handle myself just fine. That thing doesn't scare me. I've survived far worse and lived to tell the tale."

"You know I won't do that," he says. "We go in together. We come out together. End of story."

"No, Otto, you don't have to worry about me. Please. In all these years, I've had plenty of opportunities to die, and at this point, part of me is beginning to believe that I can't. That no matter what happens, I'll somehow be alright." She takes a deep breath. "Will you just promise me that you will put yourself first, and the girl first? Please?"

Otto frowns, then nods. "I... I will."

"Very well then," Dr. Brighton says.

She takes his hand and leads him across the threshold, into the dark tunnel.

Otto turns on his flashlight, but it does very little. All they can see ahead is a few measly feet. The rest is pure and unfathomable darkness.

"It's cold in here," he whispers, his voice echoing off the stone walls.

Dr. Brighton squeezes his hand again. "Stay close. And Otto?"

"Yeah?"

"If we hear anything behind us, anything at all, we run. No matter what's ahead, we run toward it. Because whatever is behind us will be worse."

CHAPTER 16

Traitors

Once his feet cross the threshold, Otto realises that, for the first time in his adult life, he is afraid of the dark. He grips the flashlight tightly with one hand while the other stays poised, ready to grab the rifle at any moment. The tunnel is cold and echoey, with a dirt floor scattered with dozens of tracks. Some are large footprints, just like John's. Others are small, animal-like. And some are unmistakably human.

Maybe Sandy isn't the only victim.

Or maybe it's just the two kids law enforcement spotted in the woods.

But surely, if those boys had come this far into the tunnel, they would have told the officers about the strange display of taxidermied abominations at the tunnel's entrance. Wouldn't they?

As Otto and Dr. Brighton continue down the tunnel, neither of them says a word. They focus on the beam of the flashlight, which sometimes shakes more than it should. Otto can't help it. He's nervous. Nervous about what lies at the end of this rabbit hole.

Nervous they won't find Sandy alive.

And more than that, nervous they'll find something worse than a dead Sandy. Because if Otto has learned anything since he first encountered evil, it's that there are things far worse than death. That there are evils so sinister, so demonic, that sometimes one would beg for death rather than endure the world's most wicked afflictions.

"Do you see that?" Dr. Brighton whispers, breaking the silence. She grabs his arm, making him jump.

He narrows his eyes and squints down the tunnel, which seems to stretch for miles.

"Look," Dr. Brighton says again, clutching his jacket.

And then he sees it.

Faint in the distance, a yellow glow slowly permeates the darkness up ahead.

"Someone else is down here," Dr. Brighton murmurs. "That's a flashlight."

Otto watches the faint light grow stronger. They will soon collide with whoever, or whatever, is in the tunnels.

"We should say something," Dr. Brighton whispers.

He nods as they continue walking. The tunnel seems to descend deeper into the heart of Jericho Mountain. With each step, the air grows colder, a grim reminder that there is only one way out, the same way they came in.

"H-Hello?" Otto calls, his voice shaking. It echoes through the cavern, sending chills down his spine.

Only silence answers.

"Who is down there?" he asks again.

Still, no reply.

He quickly turns to Dr. Brighton. "Should we turn around?"

Dr. Brighton shakes her head and lowers her voice to a whisper. "No. We'll find out soon enough who, or what, we're dealing with. Remember, we have guns." She lifts the bloodstained hatchet. "And this. We're not underprepared."

Otto nods. He hands Dr. Brighton the flashlight and pulls the rifle off his shoulder, holding it ready to fire at a moment's notice.

As they walk further down the tunnel, they slowly begin to see who is approaching them. It's a tall man, maybe six and a half feet. He wears a tattered white shirt and looks like he has been in the caves for days. His jeans are too short, falling just above his ankles, and his feet drag along the ground as if they are too heavy for him to lift.

He appears unarmed. Expressionless, except for the wave of exhaustion that stains his face.

"Who are you?" Otto asks once they are within a safe distance.

The man lets out a small smile, revealing a row of crooked teeth stained a deep brown. Each tooth is a different size, jutting out like broken dominoes, twisted every which way in his gums.

"Are you the Mayor?" the man asks in a low, hoarse voice.

Otto swallows hard and nods. "Yes."

"Oh!" the man exclaims, smiling wide. His skin is grey and pale, caked with dirt. "Great. Great news. You did it! We knew you would. You've made such great strides. Hurrah! You've found the missing girl. Or you're about to."

"Take me to her," Otto says, raising his rifle. "Or I will shoot."

The man raises his hands above his head, tilting his flashlight toward the ceiling of the cave. "Yes, yes. Of course. I shall. But do tell me, who is this lovely old woman you've brought with you? I wasn't expecting company. No... that wasn't part of the plan."

"What plan?" Dr. Brighton growls.

The man smiles. "How rude of me not to introduce myself. You see, my name is Nicholas. Nicholas Brown."

Otto narrows his eyes. The name sounds vaguely familiar.

"I asked, what plan?" Dr. Brighton repeats, firmer this time.

Nicholas jumps. "A feisty one! The plan. Yes, the plan was very simple, if I remember it correctly. And if I don't, please be patient with me. It's been a long... life."

Otto grips his gun tighter. He's not sure whether he should shoot the man or let him keep talking.

"The plan. Divide the group. Get the Mayor here on his own because he must 'save Sandy.' Except... the Mayor isn't here alone."

"So, you knew Chief Lavoie would go try to find John?" Otto asks.

Nicholas nods ferociously, too happy, too eager.

"And Marie?" Dr. Brighton asks.

"Mrs. Lavoie," Nicholas coos. "She would never hurt her favorite son. Silly of you to think that."

Otto's heart pounds in his chest. Clementine. She's with Marie, all alone. And judging by the smile on Nicholas's face, it sounds like Marie never had any intention of helping them at all.

"But you, this other old woman. We didn't account for you. Why are you here?" Nicholas asks.

Dr. Brighton takes a step forward and narrows her eyes, squinting into the darkness. "Marie. Did she know about this?"

Otto snaps his head toward Dr. Brighton. Marie? A traitor?

Nicholas grins, baring his wretched, piano-key teeth like an animal. "That's for me to know and for you to find out."

CHAPTER 17

Concerning Patterns of Behavior

When Clementine first saw Marie break down in front of the group, she felt a flicker of sympathy for the old woman. She wasn't sure why, but it was enough to agree to bring her back to the house, where John and Chief Lavoie were likely feuding. That is, if Chief Lavoie was lucky enough to still be alive to tell the tale.

The farther they walked, the more anxious Clementine became. A creeping sense of dread grew with every step, warning her that she might be walking straight into a trap.

The images of the Fool, of John, came rocketing back to her. His sinister smile when he looked at Lily like she was a piece of meat instead of a scared little girl. The way his body didn't even flinch when Clementine fired bullets into his chest.

The closer she and Marie got to the Lavoie house on the edge of the woods, the more Clementine wanted to turn around and run back toward Otto.

And it wasn't just the memories.

Something else was making her feel unsettled.

Marie was no longer moving like an old woman. She wasn't stumbling over branches or gingerly stepping over tree trunks like they were live wires. Now she was moving quickly, with purpose. In fact, Clementine had been guiding her the entire way into the woods, making sure she didn't fall behind or get lost.

Now, Marie was leading the way with newfound intensity. It was as if she had walked this path dozens of times before. As if she knew the exact way from the clearing to her house.

At first, Clementine said nothing. She just mulled the oddities over in her mind.

But the moment she saw the house on the horizon, she stopped dead in her tracks.

Marie didn't notice at first. She kept walking toward the house, only pausing when she realized Clementine was no longer following.

"Come on," Marie said. "We're almost there."

Clementine shakes her head. "No. I'm going to leave you here. I need to go back and make sure that Otto is okay."

Marie frowns and throws her hands in the air. "No. I need you to come with me. What if... what if something happened to Nolan or John? I... I can't make it the rest of the way by myself. I'm old, you see."

Clementine bites her bottom lip and crosses her arms over her chest. "Why do you want me to go with you so badly?"

Marie shrugs. "I... there's safety in numbers."

"It wasn't my idea to come back here," Clementine says. "I did what I told you I would do. I brought you back to the house. Now you're on your own."

"But I need you to help me! To ward off John while I say the spell. To turn him back, you know. I can't do that on my own. What if Nolan is hurt? I need someone smart and strong to hold John back if he—"

Clementine shakes her head. Her braids sway in the slow spring breeze as the sun begins to peek over the horizon.

"You were never going to say the spell, Marie," she says. "I'm not stupid."

Marie takes a step toward her, and Clementine quickly draws her gun, raising it and pointing it at Marie's chest.

"You wouldn't," Marie whispers.

Clementine swallows hard. "I would. I don't trust you. Tell me why you could barely walk when we brought you out into the woods, and now you lead me here like you know exactly where you're going. No hesitation. No struggle. I don't believe you."

Marie hems and haws, but Clementine cuts her off.

"Turn around. Go back to the house. Check on your sons, and leave me be."

Marie nods slowly. "And... you won't hurt me?"

In that moment, something primal takes over Clementine, the raw instinct to survive. In all her training and field work with the FBI, one lesson has been hammered in over and over: kill them before they have the chance to kill you.

And right now, even if she can't explain it, she feels it deep in her bones, a warning. A pressure in her chest that tells her she is in grave danger.

She nods, lowering her gun. "Just go."

Marie nods in return and turns away.

The moment she does, Clementine raises her weapon and fires, one clean shot to the back of Marie's head. The crack of the gunshot tears through the quiet forest like a whip.

Marie collapses face-first onto the earth, lifeless.

Little did Clementine know, that single bullet would unleash a storm of vengeance none of them were prepared to face.

CHAPTER 18

Revelations

D r. Brighton can't put her finger on it, but something feels very off about this Nicholas character they've met in the tunnels. It's not just that he's an accomplice of John, lurking in the shadows of a dark tunnel in the middle of the forest, his movements seem off too.

She tries to focus. To think. But Otto's loud attempt to take control of the situation distracts her.

"Take us to Sandy," Otto yells. "Now. No more games. You bring us to her, and no one gets hurt."

Nicholas nods and rubs his hands together. "Taking you to Sandy was always my intention. Just follow me."

He turns and walks down the tunnel, glancing back briefly to beckon them with a quick tilt of his hand.

Otto and Dr. Brighton exchange concerned looks, but Otto takes the lead and begins to follow him.

Dr. Brighton trails behind, gripping her axe and glancing over her shoulder every few moments.

What if something's behind them? What if it's John?

Her heart races in her chest, yet a strange sense of calm washes over her. She's completely, utterly prepared to sacrifice herself at any moment, for Otto or for Sandy. After decades of chasing the bizarre, the occult, and the macabre, surely she can't die in these tunnels. That would be... embarrassing.

After all the danger she's faced, all the creatures she's confronted, after literally surviving Hell itself, being killed in the lair of an overgrown rabbit would be a joke.

For a moment, Dr. Brighton imagines dying and arriving in Hell, face-to-face with the Devil himself, laughing.

"You died at the hands of a Fool?"

Oh, He would never let her live it down.

You see, Dr. Brighton knows she's going to Hell. There's no escaping it. It's why she has the mark on her hand, that gaping, ugly scar that reminds her of the day she sacrificed her only life, ten years ago, to save the masses. She's not proud of it, but she did what had to be done.

Yet, in a strange way, her complete and utter damnation makes her feel not just protected, but invincible. She's made it this far, she can't be killed by an overgrown rabbit.

And that's when she notices it.

It's like a light bulb going off in her brain.

Nicholas' elongated stature.

His massive feet.

Those ears, too large for a human head, almost like a circus monkey's.

That botched smile that doesn't sit right.

Dr. Brighton grabs Otto by the arm, trying to mouth to him what her brain is screaming. He looks at her, confused, as they continue following Nicholas down the dark tunnel.

"What?" Otto whispers. "I don't understand."

"Secrets don't make friends!" Nicholas coos from ahead. He doesn't even turn around.

His hearing is sharp. Exactly as Dr. Brighton imagined.

Nicholas, like John, is a Fool. And like John, he didn't complete the full transformation. From the little Dr. Brighton has studied about these bizarre creatures, she knows one thing for certain: the Fool spell is meant for children, and only children. When parents or other witches have tried to perform the spell on adults... the results have been mixed. Some don't survive the process. Others sprout white hair all over their bodies but undergo no other changes. And then there are a select few who turn out like Nicholas, humanlike, but with distorted proportions, forced to live in shame and shadow.

Still, Dr. Brighton keeps it to herself. The only thing worse than Otto not knowing that Nicholas is likely ten times stronger than they anticipated is Nicholas realizing that they know. Because then, he'll understand that Dr. Brighton isn't just some ordinary old woman.

She's a much bigger threat.

And while she and Otto may be two lambs walking into the depths of the tunnel toward slaughter, Dr. Brighton holds the key to ending all of this madness, right there in her pocket.

The Fool spell.

She had intended to use it on Marie, but now there's a chance she'll have to attempt it all on her own. She's not a witch, but that's never stopped her before. Sometimes, things just have a way of working out for her in the most dire situations. Maybe it's God. Maybe it's the Devil. Either way, Dr. Brighton believes she can put an end to this nightmare, with or without Marie.

If only she truly believes she can.

Then again, a non-witch performing a spell like this is dangerous. It could kill John. It could kill Nicholas. It could even kill the witch who dares to reverse it. But for some reason, there's a pull in her heart that tells her she'll be alright.

As long as she believes it.

After what feels like ages of walking, Nicholas brings them to a tall door that reaches the full height of the tunnel. By now, they've been walking so long that the passage has gradually narrowed, shrinking tighter and shorter, until Nicholas has to bow his head just to move through it.

The door resembles something you'd find on a ship: tall, metal, with a circular wheel in the center used to unlock and open it.

"How long have you been down here?" Otto asks, still gripping the gun, ready to fire at the first sign of aggression.

Nicholas smiles and begins turning the wheel. "A long time. John is a long-time friend."

"What does that mean?" Otto asks.

Nicholas pauses mid-turn and glances back at him. "When Mrs. Lavoie did... what she did to John, I lost my best friend, the only person in this world who ever understood me. Everyone in town said he ran away. And then, one day, I noticed these yellow eyes watching me from the woods at night. I don't know why, but I decided to go down there and look. And it was John. At first, he was afraid to show himself, after all of his... changes. But he told me he was lonely. And scared. So I followed him."

"You followed him here?" Otto presses.

Nicholas nods and resumes turning the wheel until it locks with a dull, unsatisfying click. "They used to mine mica here, years ago. No one's been down here in ages. So we made it our own."

He begins to open the door, but Otto stops him.

"Wait," he says.

Nicholas freezes, turning slowly to look at him with his grey, vacant eyes.

"Why Sandy?" Otto asks quietly. "Why couldn't you just leave her alone? She's just a little girl."

Nicholas shrugs and takes a deep breath. "I have no power over John, okay? He's stronger than me. He could kill me with sheer brute force if he wanted to. I told him to stay away from her. But he said that if he took her, he might finally get what he really wants."

"And what is that?" Otto presses.

Nicholas exhales again and shakes his head. "Honest answer?"

Otto nods and raises the rifle slightly.

"Your daughter."

The next few moments unfold in a blur. Otto, seized by fury, cocks the gun, but Dr. Brighton lets out a sharp yelp. She drops the hatchet and throws her hand over the barrel.

"Don't," she says, gripping it firmly and pushing it away from Nicholas.

Otto trembles, barely able to pull the trigger even if he wanted to.

"Smart," Nicholas murmurs.

"You won't win this fight, Otto," Dr. Brighton says gently. "Please. Just trust me."

Otto grimaces and jerks the rifle free from her grip, pointing it back at Nicholas. "Take us to Sandy. Now."

Nicholas nods. "As you wish."

He pushes the door open, revealing a vast, dark room with towering ceilings. Dim candlelight flickers across the stone walls, casting shadows that make the space resemble a dungeon.

As Otto and Dr. Brighton step across the threshold, they see horrors beyond their wildest imagination.

CHAPTER 19

Presents

It wasn't long after Clementine fired the gun that she realised she'd made a grave mistake. When the sound of the gunshot echoed through the forest and bounced back at her, she stood frozen, gun still in hand, as a series of nerve-racking truths settled in.

Marie had likely led her here on purpose, straight to her own demise.

She'd just killed the only person in the woods who had the ability to reverse the Fool spell, although, deep down, Clementine doubted Marie ever intended to use it.

And, perhaps most troubling of all, the gunshot had echoed louder than she'd hoped. Whatever, or whoever, that creature was, it had definitely heard it.

So, the moment Marie's body hits the forest floor with a sickening thud, Clementine doesn't wait. She doesn't rush to check if the witch is dead. She holsters the gun and takes off running, retracing her steps through the trees.

She runs faster than she has in years, whispering prayers to God that she never has to see that repulsive creature again. Maybe it's all her years of government training, or a decade spent navigating bureaucracy, but Clementine just can't wrap her head around any of this.

Witches?

Rabbit cryptids?

It's absurd. And yet, here she is, sprinting through the woods, leaping over sticks and tree trunks, running from something that shouldn't exist, something that's managed to turn her life upside down in just forty-eight hours.

All she can do is hope.

Hope that maybe the creature isn't as terrible as she remembers.

Hope that maybe it can be beaten with bullets.

Hope that, just maybe, she didn't try hard enough last night.

Her mind floods with thoughts. Shadows of doubt creep in. Maybe this isn't as bad as they all feared. Maybe she could take on John, or the Fool, or whatever it is, all on her own.

When she passes through the wretched curtain of hanging squirrels and reaches the clearing, she stops running. Her lungs burn with exhaustion as she bends forward, gasping for breath.

The only sound in the forest is the echo of her exasperated breathing, carried through the trees.

Once she catches her breath, she straightens and looks up. The darkness is beginning to lift, and the stars are fading from the sky.

Then she hears it, a wet, rolling sound, like a ball being kicked through the mud.

Clementine lowers her gaze from the sky and turns toward the edge of the clearing. Something is rolling toward her. At first, she can't tell what it is. It's round, about the size of a basketball, and it bounces awkwardly over sticks and leaves, lopsided and deliberate.

Then she sees it clearly.

It's Chief Lavoie's head.

His eyes are wide open, staring up at her with absolute terror. His face is matted with blood, and his mouth hangs open as if he died mid-scream. The base of his neck is jagged and torn, ripped, not cleanly cut.

Clementine stumbles backward and lets out a scream that echoes through the clearing.

That's when she hears the laughter.

It starts as a low chuckle from somewhere in the bushes, but then it grows louder, more unhinged, like whoever is laughing can't stop. The sound bounces around the clearing, coming from all directions, making it impossible for Clementine to tell where John is hiding.

"Did you like my present?" John's voice calls from the darkness. It's sing-songy. Playful. Like a child. "Don't worry about the body. I'm saving that for something special."

Clementine narrows her eyes. In the distance, across the clearing, she spots them, yellow eyes glowing from deep within the brush. Without hesitation, she draws her gun and fires a round, praying that whatever that sick creature is will drop just like its mother did.

But it doesn't.

Instead, the creature steps out from the bushes with a grin that sends a chill down her spine. It towers over the clearing, reminding her that it's stronger, faster, and more powerful than she'll ever be.

She starts backing up, slowly, as John approaches. His long feet drag across the forest floor, leaving a trail in the dirt behind him.

"You know what I'm going to do with fat little Nolly's head?" John says, smiling. He bares his teeth with an almost cat-like hiss, eyes locked on hers.

She says nothing.

"I'm going to put his head on the fattest pig I can find," John continues. "Because that's all he ever was, wasn't he? A fat little piggy playing dress-up in his police uniform." He giggles and claps his hands together like a delighted child. "All those years he thought he was so important. Chief of Police. But really, he was just a scared little pig who couldn't even save himself. I'll put him on my front lawn, and every day I'll walk by and pat him on the head. He'll be such a great addition to my... collection."

Clementine keeps walking backward, her body trembling. She fires two more bullets into the creature, but they seem to vanish into his body, absorbed without effect.

"There's no need," the creature says, smiling. "It's over. You cannot run. You cannot hide. And don't think I don't know what you did! Oh, I know. I know exactly what you did."

Clementine swallows hard, her heart pounding in her chest.

"But... I won't kill you right now. I want your friends to watch. I had to watch you kill my mother, I think it's only fair they see the same."

"You saw?" she asks.

John nods. His long ears twitch with anger as he steps toward her. "I did. And then I followed you as you ran through the woods, thinking you'd get away from me. Silly, isn't it?"

He's just feet away now. Clementine has backed up so far she's nearly at the edge of the clearing.

"So you will come with me," John says. "And we will find your friends, and they will watch as I kill you in the most brutal and ugly way I can think of. And then, you'll be part of my display. Next to Nolly. Two pigs in a pod."

Clementine tries to run, but John is faster than anything she's ever seen. His massive hand wraps around her throat, lifting her off the ground like she weighs nothing. His claws pierce her skin as he yanks her closer. His wide, twisted mouth spews a hot spray of spit in her face as he speaks.

"No more running," he whispers.

His yellow eyes glow in the dim light, and for a brief moment, Clementine sees her own terrified reflection staring back at her. The fear in her face is undeniable; raw, frozen, helpless.

"Time to go collect your friends."

And with that, John drags her deeper into the woods, his claws digging into her skin as her feet scrape against the forest floor. The trees close in around them. The path disappears beneath layers of leaves and rot.

Ahead, the tunnels wait; silent, dark, and cold, where Otto and Dr. Brighton stand unaware, still believing they have time.

They don't.

Their nightmare is about to get much, much worse.

CHAPTER 20

Trapped

When Otto steps through the door into the room, his stomach turns at the sight before him. Dr. Brighton follows close behind, clinging to his arm, her grip tight with fear.

The room resembles a cave; tall ceilings, rough stone walls, and spanning roughly a thousand square feet. The floor is dirt, and scattered across it are dozens of small white objects. At first, Otto thinks they're pebbles, or maybe bits of broken glass. But when he looks closer, his blood runs cold.

They're teeth.

He swallows hard and scans the rest of the space. The walls are lined with shelves carved directly into the rock. On each shelf sit rows of glass jars, filled with things Otto doesn't want to examine too closely. Some appear to be eyeballs. Others look like tiny fingers or toes, suspended in a murky yellow liquid.

The smell is almost unbearable. He's forced to breathe through his mouth. It reeks of death, urine, and something cloyingly sweet—so foul it makes him gag.

In the centre of the room stands a large wooden table, stained black with dried blood. Knives are strewn across its surface; some small, like fish gutting tools, others large, cleaver-like blades. All of them are crusted with dark brown residue that Otto knows isn't rust.

But it's what he sees in the back corner that makes his heart stop.

Behind a curtain of hanging animal skins, a small figure is huddled on the ground. It has white fur and long ears, but something about it looks off. Too small. Too fragile.

Otto squints into the dim candlelight, struggling to make sense of what he's seeing.

Before he can react, a loud slam erupts behind them. They whirl around.

The door they came through has closed. A metallic *click* echoes through the cave, locking them inside.

Otto rushes to the door and pounds on it with both fists.

"Nicholas!" he yells. "Nicholas, don't do this!"

"It will be okay," Nicholas replies from the other side, his voice oddly calm. "I just need to keep you here until John gets back. Then everything will be fine!"

Otto turns to Dr. Brighton, panic etched across his face.

"What do we do?"

Dr. Brighton stammers, both of them stunned, unable to believe they could have been so goddamn stupid.

Otto slams his fist against the door. "Nicholas, please! I'll give you whatever you want. Money, do you want money? If you take us to Sandy and let us go, I'll give you fifty thousand dollars. I'll give you anything! Please, just let us go!"

"I already took you to Sandy," Nicholas replies, his voice fading behind the door. "I can't give you anything else."

Dr. Brighton tugs on Otto's shoulder. "I have something to tell you, something I didn't say before because I didn't know how."

Otto turns toward her, his face desperate. "What is it?"

"Nicholas is a Fool."

His eyes widen. "What?"

He turns back to the door and starts banging on it again in frustration. Dr. Brighton glances over her shoulder, eyes drifting back toward the figure in the far corner of the room. It hasn't moved.

She grabs Otto again, her voice urgent. "Listen. The Fool spell only works on children. If you try it on someone who isn't a child, the result is... deformed. That's why Nicholas is so long and lanky, and strange."

"Why would that happen?"

"I... I don't know," she says truthfully, her voice shaky. She takes a step back and looks again toward the corner.

Otto lowers his hands from the door, spiraling. "Would Marie do this? And what does he mean he already took us to Sandy? Where is she?"

Dr. Brighton doesn't answer.

She's staring now, frozen, heart sinking, at the small white figure in the corner. Her face goes pale, eyes wide with horror.

"Dr. Brighton?" Otto says, following her gaze. "What is it? What's wrong?"

He turns to look where she's looking.

The creature shifts slightly, just enough for Otto to see it more clearly.

It's about three feet tall, covered in pure white, matted fur. Long rabbit ears hang down past its shoulders.

"I don't understand, what is it?" Otto asks, his voice cracking as he tries to reason it out. "Some poor animal they tortured?"

"Otto," Dr. Brighton whispers, her voice trembling. "Look at its eyes."

Otto squints through the dim light. The creature slowly turns toward him... and then he sees them.

Blue eyes. Bright. Innocent. Terrified.

"No," Otto breathes, stumbling back. "No, that's not... that can't be..."

"The spell only works on children, Otto," Dr. Brighton says, grabbing his arm. "When they turn a child into a Fool, this is what happens. They become mute. They become more rabbit than human. When the spell is used on adults, the result is more human than rabbit. But this... this is what happens to a child."

Otto shakes his head violently. "That's not Sandy. Sandy is somewhere else. Sandy is—"

"Otto, look at her eyes!" Dr. Brighton shouts. "Don't be foolish!"

The creature tilts its head with a small, confused expression. Its mouth opens and closes, but no sound comes out. And those eyes, those beautiful blue eyes that used to light up when she saw Lily at school, are now filled with fear. And recognition.

Otto's knees buckle. He sinks to the ground, voice barely a whisper. "Sandy?"

The thing that was Sandy Sommers starts to crawl toward him, inching forward on trembling limbs, but then stops. She cowers, shrinking back, like a creature trained not to move. Trained to stay hidden.

"She can't speak, Otto," Dr. Brighton says, tears streaming down her cheeks. "Fools can't speak. But she can still think. She can still remember. Somewhere inside that body... a little girl is trapped."

TO BE CONTINUED.

AUTHOR'S NOTE

Thank you so much for reading Beater Cottontail. The third [and likely final] installment of Bunny Foo Foo will come out this March. You can pre-order it now and keep in touch with me on Instagram @evdean_author. I love hearing from readers so always feel free to shoot me a message there. And I always appreciate reviews on Goodreads and Amazon. It keeps me going!

A SNEAK PEEK AT
THE PUMPKIN FEST RIOT

This winter, I will be releasing my first full length horror novel, **The Pumpkin Fest Riot**. It takes place in small town New Hampshire in the late nineties as Beatrix, Otto, and their friend Lucy confront an ancient evil that has taken over their community. I have included the first two chapters in this book. I hope you enjoy them and you can pre-order the full book on Amazon now!

THE PUMPKIN FEST RIOT

PROLOGUE

1984 – Kensington, England

Dr. Beatrix Brighton

"Well, I certainly don't want it," says Dr. Cecilia Marshall as she crosses her arms over her chest. Her short, peppery hair sways as she shakes her head in fury.

My stomach turns as I look around the long wooden table in the middle of Dr. Winston Mercer's posh home in Kensington. There are a bunch of us here, sitting around the table, all nervous about what's about to happen.

"Well," Dr. Mercer says at the head of the table. "Someone has to take it. Someone has to keep it safe. This is not about *who wants* to take the stone. It's about *who is willing* to keep this precious artifact out of the wrong hands. To keep it safe."

Dr. Mercer looks around the room at our colleagues. Contemporaries, really. All of us are experts in the same vein of the macabre. Some are historians, some are demonologists, psychics, experts in Catholicism. We're all here to keep the Stone of One Thousand Souls from falling into the wrong hands.

"No one wants to step up to the plate?" Dr. Mercer says with a low growl. He looks toward the end of the table, where an older Spanish gentleman is staring down at his hands. "Oscar, surely you can keep it with you in Boadilla?

No?"

Oscar shakes his head and continues to look down at his hands.

No one wants it.

The stone is said to be evil. Pure evil.

Legends claim that you can feel the energy pulsing off it, filling anyone who touches it with immediate dread. One professor near the end of the table, I don't know his name, claims that you even feel a jolt of electricity when you hold it. Like it's alive.

Another man, closer to the middle of the table, claimed he saw the artifact at the home of its previous owner and accidentally inhaled some of the black, flaky dust that encrusted the rock. He fell ill and was in the hospital with severe pneumonia for two months. He was only a young and spry twenty-nine years old.

No one wants the stone.

"The stone is likely to auction in Rome next week for around 1.3 million pounds," Dr. Mercer says. "Money is not the concern. I will handle the money. But I need someone to keep it safe. Someone who will see it every morning. Someone who will make sure this stone is safe."

Silence fills the room.

I too have no interest in the stone. After all, I am just a young demonologist. I can't even believe that I was invited to this meeting in the first place. I'm honored, I guess. But I don't know anything about keeping a cursed artifact safe. I barely have a house to put it in, really.

I'm American, but I've been traveling around Europe for the past few years, doing what young people in their twenties do. Enjoying life, working here and there, and exploring the world.

Being tied down by a highly dangerous rock is not on my to-do list.

"Well, if no one is brave enough to take this on, I suggest we do what good academics do," Dr. Mercer says with a soft smile. He reaches into the leather bag that hangs on the back of his chair and fiddles around, searching for something.

"I really hoped that it wouldn't come to this, but if none of you want to volunteer to take on this responsibility, we will have to draw straws."

When Dr. Mercer holds the straws in the air, tension fills the room, and my stomach turns.

Draw straws? Like in middle school?

As he begins to walk around the table, offering straws to each of the experts here, something in my heart knows. It just knows. It knows that I am going to draw the smallest straw.

It knows that I am going to go to Rome.

It knows that I am going to be tasked with guarding the Stone of One Thousand Souls, and *it knows that I am going to fail.*

Somewhere in the back of my mind, I hear my mother's voice: "*You're too reckless to be trusted with something precious."*

I've never thought of myself as the keeper of anything sacred. I'm a bit impulsive, loud, drawn to adventure. And yet, I can't help but wonder what it would feel like to be *trusted*. To be important enough that someone chooses you.

That fleeting, stupid little thought vanishes the moment Mercer hands me the smallest straw.

THE PUMPKIN
FEST RIOT

Yankee Magazine, Haunted New England Edition October 1st, 2000

On October 31st, 1998, the small town of Robin, New Hampshire, turned into a national news story when its family-friendly Pumpkin Fest became a full-fledged riot. Cars burned in the streets, pets were murdered by rioters, and occultists chanted charms in hopes of bringing back the devil. What was once a quaint New Hampshire town became a war zone.

To this day, experts have conflicting opinions on what caused the event to spiral into chaos. Some blame the drunk college kids who flooded the streets from nearby frat parties. Others point to the Wiccan occultist who was arrested that day. A few even claim the crowd had been drinking apple cider laced with a hint of botulism that sent them into a frenzy.

Since that harrowing day, Robin has not held another Pumpkin Fest. What was once a festive fall tradition for the western part of the state is now remembered as one of the most bizarre incidents in regional history.

Since 1998, the town of Robin has canceled all Halloween events. There is no pumpkin festival, no pumpkin carving, no trick-or-treating, no apple cider. In fact, the Office of the Mayor will issue a citation if you're even seen wearing black and orange on All Hallows' Eve.

If you ask the townspeople of Robin what happened that day, many will avert their gaze. They'll shrug and say, "I don't know," before quickly pivoting to talk about how beautiful the fall foliage is this time of year. More than anything, this town wants to move on from its darkest day.

But if you're looking for a scare this Halloween, and you're not afraid of a little hocus pocus, stop by the large metal clock on Main Street. It's where the occultist, Dr. Beatrix Brighton, claims she saw the devil himself on that dark day.

While Dr. Brighton is world-renowned in her field, her views on this subject have come under scrutiny from colleagues, university administration, and the media.

You see, Dr. Brighton doesn't believe this peculiar incident was caused by drunk college kids or tainted cider. She believes it was the Devil himself making his mark on the world on his favorite day of the year.

CHAPTER 1

The Stone Of One Thousand Souls

Robin, New Hampshire 1998

Robin, New Hampshire, was a small town with little mischief until the fall of 1998. The people were polite, the students were relatively boring compared to most college campuses, and life in the town was generally uneventful. It was the kind of town you'd love to live in if you were married, had children, and wanted a quiet life.

It was pretty damn boring.

Hunter Tanner, a six-foot-tall baseball player from Medford, Massachusetts, was one of the city's bored residents. A senior and one of the oldest in his fraternity, he had stayed back two years. One year was for academics, the other for athletics. He was tired of the sleepy town of Robin and was in need of a little Halloween trickery.

Like most college students, he also needed money.

Late one night in late October, Hunter put on a black ski mask and gloves and tiptoed out of his fraternity house, heading toward the Smith Building. It was where Robin State College held all of its arts and humanities classes. And because no real mischief ever happened in Robin, the door to the building had been left unlocked. It was a quiet town with good-natured people. Nothing strange or bizarre had ever happened in Robin.

Hunter walked through the empty hallways, looking for one classroom in particular: Dr. Beatrix Brighton's history room. The door to that room was, unfortunately, locked. But that did not stop Hunter Tanner. Desperate times call for desperate measures.

In his jacket pocket, Tanner had a metal stake. He placed it against the window of the door and hit the flat side hard with the back of his hand, causing the glass to shatter across the floor. He reached through the broken pane and opened the door from the inside.

Dr. Brighton's classroom was a cabinet of curiosities, where taxidermied jackalopes shared shelf space with jars of deadly nightshade. Though kind, the history professor had an unsettling fascination with the historic and valuable oddities that made her lectures unforgettable.

Hunter Tanner, while popular with his fraternity and on campus, was a bit down on his luck. His father had passed away last year, and his mother did not work, cutting off his monthly allowance. With the demands of baseball, he didn't have time for a job. Not that there were many jobs in Robin anyway.

So he had another idea.

He was fascinated with the growth of the internet and a new thing that had just come out called eBay. You could sell anything online to anywhere in the world. And people were paying big money for the strange, the unusual, and the peculiar.

In the back of Dr. Brighton's classroom was a glass case that held her most prized possession, and what Hunter rightly assumed would be the most valuable. To someone like you or me, it would look like just a plain old giant rock. It was gray, with black dust powdering it like a sugary donut. It was propped up on a small stand in the middle of the glass box next to a sign that read:

"The Stone of One Thousand Souls."

The description read as follows:

"The Stone of One Thousand Souls was given to Queen Mary II after the Glorious Revolution by a demonologist by the name of Braxton Heritage.

*Heritage claimed that the stone had absorbed every
demonic entity that caused the strife in England for
the prior 50 years."*

Dr. Brighton talked about the stone constantly. She had acquired it from an auction in Rome a few years ago and had paid a pretty penny for it. As Hunter stared at the seemingly normal rock, he noticed that the dust gave it a bit of a glimmer. It sparkled in the darkness.

With his gloves on, Hunter delicately lifted the glass box and set it down on the ground. With his right hand, he grabbed the rock. It was about the size of a grapefruit, and it felt heavier than it should have in his hand. He slipped it into his coat pocket as some of the black dust fell onto the floor of the classroom.

Success.

He wondered how much he would start the bidding at.

Was $1,000 too high?

With $1,000, he could fix his car and even afford to give some money to his mother. And who's to say the bidding would stop there? In a few days, Hunter could be a thousandaire. Maybe even a hundred thousandaire if things went his way.

Even if Hunter had a momentary pang of guilt, it didn't last long. He justified his theft with one simple and very true fact: *Dr. Brighton had plenty of unusual and rare, expensive objects. It was only fair that Hunter had one too.*

With a skip in his step, he left Dr. Brighton's classroom and closed the door behind him.

Little did he know, he was actually carrying the weight of one thousand souls in his varsity jacket pocket.

CHAPTER 2

Demons

I sit on the edge of my brown desk as my nails dig into the rough wood. I can't believe it. The stone is gone.

I look out into my classroom filled with a bunch of students in their late teens and early twenties. I'm a professor of history at Robin State College, a small school nestled in the western part of New Hampshire. It's not the best job, but it's a job. Most of my students are pretty great. I keep to myself, and I have few problems.

Until today.

When I walked into my classroom this morning, I found the glass window on the door busted open, with shards scattered everywhere. Someone had broken into my office.

I'm not your average history professor, and I have a collection of *strange* and *unusual* artifacts that call my classroom home.

One of those artifacts is (now was) the *Stone of One Thousand Souls*. Priceless. Expensive. Dangerous. When I brought it home from Rome almost fourteen years ago, I didn't know what to do with the cursed rock.

Everywhere I brought it, it caused me pain. So when I moved to New Hampshire to start this new job at Robin State, I figured I'd keep it in the back of my classroom, guarded by thick glass, tucked away with all of my other strange and unusual things.

I didn't want that goddamn thing in my house. Not after what it had caused. After all, Robin is a sleepy, safe town with almost no crime whatsoever. Who would have thought my classroom would be a target?

And now, *best case scenario*, some dumb kid is walking around the college with a priceless demonic rock in his possession.

There is no way this ends well.

And it is pretty much all my fault.

I stare out into the sea of students watching me from the front of the class. I've just told them that the stone was stolen and that I'd gotten the police involved.

"It's a very precious artifact," I say as I cross my arms over my chest. "And if anyone has any idea who may have done this, please let me know. We are offering a reward of one thousand dollars for anyone who has direct information about who stole the stone."

Quickly, a hand raises in the front of the class. It's Lucy Lemon, a young and bubbly freshman from Nottingham, a small town on the eastern side of the state. She's a sweet girl, a bit of a brown-nose, but a good kid nonetheless.

"Yes, Lucy," I say.

She pushes her bright red hair behind her ears, and her face lights up. "So if we find any information that leads to finding the stone, we get one thousand dollars?"

I nod. "Yes, but please don't get yourself into any more trouble than you need to. The rock is very, very... special, and it can't fall into the wrong hands."

· · · · · · · ● · · · · · · · · ·

When I dismiss the class, Lucy hangs behind and waits for the room of students to pour out. She approaches me eagerly as I sit at my desk, thumbing through their latest paper on the American Revolution.

"Dr. Brighton," Lucy says, staring down at me with her bright green eyes. She's wearing a Disney sweatshirt and jeans and is clutching her big canvas bag. "I want to help you find the stone."

My stomach turns. While I could use the help, I'm not sure I want these kids going on any crazy missions trying to find this rock. If they touch it or come into contact with it, who knows what could happen. They could get sick or cursed just from its touch.

"Thank you, Lucy. I appreciate you being so willing to help," I say with a small smile.

Lucy shifts back and forth in her shoes with nervous excitement. "I'm going to get my friend Otto, and we're going to get to the bottom of what happened. If I could be honest, I bet it was Chucky. He's always been eyeing that stone in the back of the room," Lucy says.

Chucky is the goth boy who sits in the back of the class and doesn't speak much. But he's a great kid. He would never take the stone.

I shake my head. "No, Chucky wouldn't do that. He understands how important the stone is to me. And while Chucky may be a bit quiet in class, it's only because he has social anxiety. He's actually a very sweet boy. We shouldn't judge a book by its cover."

Lucy's cheeks turn flush. I don't mean to embarrass her, but I am growing weary of students picking on their classmates just because they are a bit *different*.

"Well," Lucy says with a shaky voice. "If you don't mind me asking, why is the stone so important to you? I only know what it says on the plaque."

I smile. "Well, Lucy, do you mind humoring me for a minute?"

Lucy nods.

"Have you ever considered that what the plaque said might be real?" With my students at Robin State, I try not to get too far into the macabre, but every now and then I enjoy giving them just a *dash of the fantastic*. Something to hold on to in a boring world. Something that gives them a glimmer of hope that life may be a bit more interesting than it seems.

Lucy frowns. "Real? Like demons getting trapped in a stone?"

I nod. "That is what the inscription says, after all. And I'm inclined to believe history. What I mean is... what if... what if the stone really did suck up one thousand souls? And now someone is walking around with it. Someone who has no clue what harm it could cause."

Lucy has always been one of my more open-minded students, but I can see her mind reeling.

"Do you know what the inside is made of, Lucy?" I ask in a low whisper.

Lucy shakes her head.

"Pure, one hundred percent gold."

Lucy laughs. "That ugly rock had gold inside?"

She's not wrong. The stone does look like a big, black, dusty potato.

"The outside is just a layer," I say. "The inside is the heart of the stone, and it's completely one hundred percent pure gold."

Lucy nods slowly. "Wow. So that's why you need it back? Because it must cost a lot of money."

"And do you know what is attracted to pure gold?"

Lucy laughs. "Women?"

I shake my head. "Demons."

Lucy's stomach drops. "Are demons even real?"

"I know it's a bit controversial, but I think so," I say. "What do you think, Lucy?"

Lucy hesitates before she leaves, standing at my desk like she wants permission. Or maybe reassurance. Kids this age are all brittle armor and bright eyes. Lucy is all instincts and boundless curiosity. A younger me, basically. Which terrifies me.

"You really don't have to help," I say, softer than I mean to. "This isn't your problem."

"But I want to," she says. "I like *weird stuff.*"

She glances down at my desk, where a half-wrapped donut sits on a napkin. It's from the good place, the one on Main Street downtown with the sourdough base and the ridiculous maple glaze. I catch her eyeing it for a second too long.

I sigh and nudge it toward her. "Take it. You'll need the sugar if you're doing investigative work."

She grins, surprised. "Really?"

"Go for it."

She cradles it like I handed her gold. "Thanks, Dr. Brighton. I'll let you know how it goes," she says as she leaves my classroom and skips off to her new adventure.

It's like watching my younger self, and it gives me chills.

Made in United States
North Haven, CT
29 August 2025

72288225R00088